"Elevator shoes?"

"I remember those." Mom spread her thumb and index finger about two inches apart. "The entire sole is two to three inches deep, so it makes the man taller. Some people call them platform shoes."

Molly giggled. "Murray will be at least two inches taller than you, baby sis."

"Great!" Tonya rolled her eyes. "Just what I need—Murray looking down his big nose at me during the entire wedding." A sudden thought hit her. "Hey, why don't you make Lane Callie's partner, and then I can walk down the aisle with Ryan?"

Callie shook her head. "Lane is not the groomsman type. He told me that our wedding was the last one he wanted to be in for a while."

"Well, he'll have to be in *mine*." Tonya threw her hands up in the air. "If I'm going to have ten or twelve bridesmaids, I'll need all the guys I can get."

Molly smirked. "Yeah, who knows? You might even have to enlist Murray."

Tonya rolled her eyes. "No way! I can guarantee that Murray Twichell will *never* be in my wedding."

DONNA REIMEL ROBINSON is a member of JOY Writers, a local critique group. As a pastor's wife, she plays the piano for their church. In her spare time, Donna enjoys sewing and reading. The Robinsons have four children, two children-in-law, and six grandchildren. They live in Denver, Colorado. Visit Donna's Web site at www.donnarobinsonbooks.com.

Books by Donna Reimel Robinson

HEARTSONG PRESENTS
HP838—For the Love of Books

The Thing about Beauty

Donna Reimel Robinson

Heartsong Presents

This book is dedicated to my Savior, Jesus Christ,
who called me to write according to His own purpose.
Also in memory of Arlene Reimel (1921–2009).
Thanks for your prayers, Mom. I miss you.

A note from the Author:
*I love to hear from my readers! You may correspond with
me by writing:*

Donna Reimel Robinson
Author Relations
PO Box 721
Uhrichsville, OH 44683

ISBN 978-1-61626-113-9

THE THING ABOUT BEAUTY

All scripture quotations are taken from the King James Version of the
Bible.

All of the characters and events in this book are fictitious. Any resemblance to actual persons, living or dead, or to actual events is purely
coincidental.

*Our mission is to publish and distribute inspirational products offering
exceptional value and biblical encouragement to the masses.*

PRINTED IN THE U.S.A.

one

"Aggie is going to kill me."

Tonya pushed down on the accelerator, driving her little red Hyundai as fast as she dared on snowy Main Street. Despite her best effort, she was going to be late for work—again.

It didn't matter that The Beauty Spot probably had zero customers on this cold Friday morning. Aggie was a stickler for promptness. So Tonya had promised to leave the house much earlier than she did yesterday.

But yesterday it wasn't snowing.

Tonya's tires slipped on a patch of ice, and she let up on the gas pedal. Why didn't Fort Lob clear the streets? They had plow trucks, and this was December in Wyoming for goodness' sake. Main Street was reduced to two sets of snowy tire tracks.

As she passed the buildings in town, the snowfall tapered off. Jim Wilkins stood outside Wilkins Grocery in his green apron, shoveling snow off the sidewalk. He waved at her. She sped past the Cattlemen's Diner and then the Trailblazer Café. Both restaurants were booming with business on this winter morning.

Horace Frankenberg, bundled in an overcoat, black gloves, and heavy boots, stood at the curb, waiting to cross the street. A blue toboggan hat covered his thinning hair. As Tonya's Hyundai approached, it looked like he would attempt the 50-yard dash right in front of her car.

"No, Horace!" She'd never be able to stop in time.

As if he heard her, Horace took a step back and waited. She waved as she sped past. That little wave would cost her on Sunday. The fifty-year-old resident bachelor of Fort Lob would corner her at church and give her a lecture about safe driving habits.

Passing *The Scout* newspaper office, she accelerated toward Elk Road. A few revolutions of her tires slipped in rebellion, but she pressed on. The clock on the dashboard signaled two minutes to nine. She was going to make it!

A blue light flashed in her eyes, and she glanced in the rearview mirror.

"Oh no!"

A Wyoming highway patrol car, lights flashing, drove behind her. With a sinking feeling in the pit of her stomach, Tonya turned right onto Bighorn Avenue and stopped, letting the engine idle. The state trooper pulled up behind her.

Tonya expelled a breath. Now she'd be late for sure. She glanced at her reflection in the rearview mirror and fluffed her hair. Her gaze roved her face, noting the perfect eyebrows she had tweezed an hour ago, the twilight shadow that shimmered on her lids and brought out the blue in her dark eyes, and the midnight mascara that separated her eyelashes perfectly. The state trooper would probably be an old married guy, but even married men gave her face a second glance.

Hopefully she could use her beauty to full advantage and get out of a speeding ticket.

Behind her the patrol car's door opened. Tonya grabbed her purse and rummaged inside for her driver's license. When a tap sounded on the tinted window, she pushed the button to roll it down. A dark green uniform came into view, and she looked up into the homely face of Murray Twichell.

"Murray!" She swiveled left to face him. "Please don't give me a ticket! I'm already late for work, and Aggie threatened to dock my pay if I was late one more day."

He raised reddish-brown eyebrows. "Maybe you should get up earlier, Tonya."

Her face grew warm. "I got up early! But it was really snowing this morning, in case you didn't notice, and it slowed me down. It's seven miles from our ranch into town, and the road was barely plowed."

Murray leaned over, folding his arms on the edge of her

window and effectively blocking the cold air that tried to swirl in. "You were going forty-eight in a thirty-five zone. On a sunny day, that would be breaking the law. On slippery, snowy roads, that's downright dangerous."

Clamping her lips shut, Tonya stared at Murray. She had always thought his blue eyes, surrounded by those reddish-brown eyelashes, were much too close together, and his nose was too big for his face. Her sister, Callie, said Murray looked like a leprechaun, but Tonya thought he looked more like a weasel.

"Furthermore," he continued, "you almost hit Horace Frankenberg."

"I did not! You should give him a ticket for jaywalking."

Murray shook his head. "I've watched you speed down Main Street for the past two weeks. I decided this morning would be the last day." He paused. "I need your driver's license, registration, and proof of insurance."

She glared at him. "Are you saying this ticket was premeditated? Kind of like premeditated murder?"

He grinned. She had never noticed how white and straight his teeth were before now. "Premeditated? You could say that." His smile faded. "Main Street is a state highway, so it's part of my duty to watch this road. Yesterday, in good weather, you must have been doing at least fifty-five. But I wasn't near my patrol car, so I couldn't chase you down." Murray shook his head. "That kind of speed could land you in court."

Yesterday she was going closer to sixty, and if it hadn't been snowing today. . .*Thank You, Lord, for the snow!* But she couldn't afford a ticket; it would increase her insurance payment.

Leaning toward him, she placed her hand on his arm, hoping Murray would notice her perfectly manicured dusty rose fingernails. "Must you give me a ticket? I've learned my lesson." She fluttered her eyelashes, trying to look pathetic and beautiful at the same time. Knowing the power of a woman's eyelashes, she was confident her charm would persuade even Murray to relent.

His gaze roamed her face a second before he straightened, pulling his arm away from her grasp. "Stop trying to act so innocent, Tonya. In the eyes of the law, you're guilty, and you've been guilty for several days. I really should give you ten speeding tickets, but I guess one will have to do."

The eyelashes didn't work! That man didn't have a romantic bone in his body. "Okay, let's make a deal."

Murray's eyebrows scrunched up. "This isn't a game show."

She spread out her hands. "If I promise to drive within the speed limit, will you let me go? And I do promise. Sincerely, I do." She glanced up at him and tried the eyelashes one more time. "Come on, Murray, you've known me since I was born."

He folded his arms. "I was only three years old when you were born, and neither one of us was driving a car back then, as I recall. Now hand over your license."

With a sigh she complied.

He took it. "You can get your registration and insurance while I process this." He walked back to his patrol car where the lights were still flashing, announcing to the entire town that she had broken the law.

Tonya hit the window button to push it up and turned the heater's fan to full blast. She wished she could blast Murray with a barrage of words. This ticket was another incident in the long list of terrible things he had done to her during her twenty-three years of life.

Well, maybe that list wasn't so long, but it had to be at least the third bad thing. She wasn't going to forgive him either.

❧

Man, that girl irked him!

With a shiver, Murray slipped into the driver's seat of his black Chevy Impala patrol car. Turning up the heater, he wished he could tell Tonya Brandt what he really thought about her. Who did she think she was—trying to use her beauty to get out of paying a speeding ticket?

Her beauty. Yep, she sure was beautiful, he had to admit

that. When she leaned toward him, her face only inches from his own, and batted those thick black eyelashes, he almost relented. Tonya rivaled most Hollywood actresses with her silky black hair, dark blue eyes, and flawless skin.

Murray had never thought much about her beauty before. Having known Tonya since childhood, he always thought of her as Callie's baby sister, the little pest who tagged after them. But now men stood in line to ask for one evening of her company. She must have dated every guy in Niobrara County.

And I can't get a date to save my life.

But what did it matter? He wasn't about to stand in line and grovel at her feet. And he wasn't going to let her get out of this speeding ticket either. She deserved it.

Picking up a clipboard, he positioned the ticket and began filling in the lines with his neat, square printing.

ঙ

"Eighty-five dollars!" Tonya sat in one of the two beautician chairs at The Beauty Spot. "Can you believe this, Aggie? Just because I drove a few miles over the speed limit, I have to pay eighty-five bucks. And I can't write out a check—no, I have to get a money order at the bank and mail it to the county courthouse in Cheyenne."

Agatha Collingsworth swept a broom under the other chair, cleaning up after their one and only customer of the morning. "Now, sugar, it's what I've been telling you for weeks." Her gold bangle bracelets clinked together as she continued sweeping. "Get your bod out of the bed when you're supposed to, and the day'll go much smoother."

"I did get up early, but Murray had determined to give me a ticket. It was premeditated."

Aggie let out a throaty chuckle as she smoothed down her pink beehive hairdo. "Premeditated, eh? More likely Murray was just doing his job."

Tonya raised her chin an inch. "I do not appreciate him watching me like that—sitting in his patrol car waiting for me to drive by and hoping I'd go a few miles over the speed limit so he could ticket me."

"Don't take it so personal." Aggie finished sweeping.

"I can't help it. I never liked Murray Twichell."

"What's wrong with him, sugar?" Aggie's dark brown eyes stared at her. "He's a nice boy."

"Nice? He's not nice. He threw a snake—a real snake—at me."

Aggie leaned on the broom handle. "He didn't!"

"Yes he did. It was a garter snake—but still, he threw it at me, and it got tangled up in my hair." A shiver ran over Tonya just thinking about it.

"That's awful, hon! When did this happen?"

Tonya tapped her lips. "I think I was seven—"

"Seven!" Aggie placed her hands on her wide hips. "Land sakes, girl. This happened when you two was little kids, and you're still holding it against him?"

Tonya felt her temper flare. "I had nightmares for weeks! If Callie hadn't managed to get that scaly thing untangled from my braids, it might still be there."

"If that don't beat all." Aggie chuckled as she waddled to the back of the store. Her tight jeans puffed out at her thighs, straining the seams.

Tonya followed her boss. "But that wasn't the only time Murray was mean to me. The summer after that, he and my brother were catching toads in the pond down at the end of our property."

Aggie chortled as she closed the storage room door. "I bet he threw a toad at you."

"It's not funny! He chased me with several toads and then stuck one down the back of my shirt."

Aggie's laughter pealed out as they made their way to the front. "He thought you were cute. It was just his boyish way of getting your attention."

"Oh, he had my attention all right." Tonya folded her arms as she dropped into a chair. "I had nightmares about that one, too."

"Don't let it eat at you." Aggie ambled toward the front door. "You have to forgive and forget."

Tonya sighed. "That won't be easy. Do you know that I had warts all over my hands when I was in the fifth grade? I think it was because of that toad." She splayed her fingers and scrutinized them. Sometimes a wart would still pop up.

Aggie looked out the large plate-glass windows. "Don't know if we'll have too many customers today. It sure is snowing." Aggie seemed ready to close the subject about Murray.

Forgive and forget. Why did Tonya still resent what he did those many years ago? Maybe what Aggie said was true—he thought she was a cute little girl and wanted her attention. Tonya had never looked at it from his point of view before.

Joining Aggie at the window, Tonya gazed out at the bleak snowy day. The snowflakes were falling hard, and the wind often swept them sideways. "We might get snowed in and have to spend the night at The Beauty Spot."

"Hope not." Aggie walked behind the cash register. "Course, it's Friday, and I need to do my bookkeeping. A couple bills to pay and your salary check to make out." Her dark eyes twinkled as she glanced at Tonya. "Do you think ya can handle the thousands of customers who'll flock to our beauty shop while I work on the books?"

Tonya smiled. "I've got it covered, Aggie. You write out those checks. Tomorrow I plan to go shopping."

"Now don't spend all your money, sugar. Remember that speeding ticket."

"You had to remind me." Tonya sighed.

The morning and afternoon dragged by with only two more customers. At four o'clock, the bell over the door jangled. Both women turned as Murray Twichell strode inside.

Tonya placed her hands on her hips. "Murray! What are you doing here?" He never came to The Beauty Spot.

Aggie had a sudden coughing fit.

His small, closely spaced eyes widened. "I need a haircut."

He shook the snow off his heavy jacket and hung it on one of the hooks on the wall.

Of all the people to want a haircut! The overpowering fragrance of his aftershave wafted toward her, and Tonya resisted the urge to sneeze. He must have just splashed some on his face before he walked in. His reddish-brown hair was growing down the back of his neck, but the top seemed kind of short, almost like a crew cut. *He wouldn't look so bad if he let his hair grow in the front.* But she wasn't going to argue about cutting his hair. After all, he was a paying customer.

Murray turned around and cracked his knuckles. "Clint's Barbershop is closed today. Must be the snow."

Without replying, Tonya walked back to her workstation. She pulled the vinyl cape off the chair and waited as he approached.

Obviously Murray was off duty. His state trooper uniform had been exchanged for old jeans and a navy T-shirt that stretched across his chest. His biceps bulged out of the short sleeves.

Wow, he's really bulked up. She remembered him as the skinny kid catching toads with Derek. Murray had towered over her back then, but now he seemed short and stocky. Callie said he was only five feet six inches. Tonya was an inch taller.

He took a seat, and Tonya threw the cape around his shoulders. With the slight movement of air, the overpowering aftershave floated toward her. She grabbed her nose so she wouldn't sneeze, taking a deep breath through her mouth. When the feeling passed, she snapped the cape together at the back of his neck. "Don't blame me if I nip your ear or—or accidentally cut off your head."

Aggie had another coughing fit.

"Still upset about that ticket?" Murray's eyes met Tonya's in the mirror. "I'm a professional who did my job, Tonya. Now you need to do yours."

"You could have let me go." She took her spray bottle

and doused his hair with water, wishing she could wash the aftershave off his face. "That would have been the Christian thing to do, in my humble opinion."

"Are you sure it's humble?" He closed his eyes against the onslaught of water.

As the water dripped from his head, Tonya's conscience hit her. *This is ridiculous.* She was a professional, as Murray said, but she was acting like a spoiled child.

It was all that toad's fault.

Forgive and forget. Grabbing a towel, she mopped up some of the water. "Okay, how do you want your hair cut?" She would give Murray the best haircut he ever had, and somehow—but only with a divine miracle—she would improve his looks in the process.

two

With a flourish, Tonya wrote her name on the 3 x 5 card. She added, *I love old movies, the colors blue and purple, and classical music.* She handed the card to her brother, Derek, who collected a card from each member of the Sunday school class. The single people of the church, comprised mainly of women, attended this class, known as the Single Servings. Most of the members were in their twenties or thirties, although Horace Frankenberg attended, as did Aggie, Tonya's boss. Aggie must be over sixty-five. She was always threatening to retire.

"Do I have everyone's card?" Derek's eyes circled the seventeen chairs. "Now here's the reason I'm collecting this information. Our class has been studying Christian charity and friendship during the past two months, and for the next six weeks, from Christmas until Valentine's Day, we're going to show some of that friendship by doing something totally different." He cleared his throat. "Everyone is going to get a secret pal."

"Secret pal?" several voices asked in unison, followed by moans—mainly in the bass timbre—and an outbreak of conversation.

A little thrill shot through Tonya at Derek's great idea. She looked around. Why all the complaining? She loved secrets, and what could be more fun than secret pals? Smoothing her red skirt, she crossed her legs, letting her black stiletto-heeled boot swing back and forth. She looked at her brother, thankful that once he made up his mind, he usually didn't change it.

Derek held up his hand. "Yes, we're going to do this. Sometimes single people get lonely and need encouragement, especially over the holidays. That's where Christian charity comes in."

"But I don't get it." Corey Henning folded his arms across

14

his lanky torso. "Are we supposed to send flowers to the other person or something?"

"Yeah." Matthew Werth slid down an inch in his seat. "What do we have to do?"

Derek straightened his tie. "Send that person a card in the mail to encourage him or her. Pray for that person every day, and let them know you're praying. You could even send a gift, or several gifts, if you want."

Corey smirked. "What if we don't want?"

Tonya glared at him. "Don't be a party pooper, Corey. It's only for six weeks."

She hoped she didn't get Corey or Matthew as a secret pal. She had dated each of them one time, and once was enough. All Corey wanted to do was kiss her, and Matthew had barely said a word.

On the other hand. . .Tonya glanced across the room at Reed Dickens—the hottest guy in the Single Servings, and she had never dated him. Of course, he had only been attending their church a few weeks. He worked at the county hospital in Lusk and, she wasn't sure, but he might be a doctor.

"All right." Derek lifted his hand to stop the undercurrent of chitchat. "Let's try it out and see what happens. This week I'll select—at random—a secret pal for everyone. I'll give these cards back next week, and remember to keep that person's name to yourself. As a secret pal, you need to encourage and pray for your, uh, person." He grinned. "I'm not sure what the recipient of a secret pal is called."

"How about your chosen one?" Horace called out.

Tonya rolled her eyes. She sure hoped she didn't get Horace. Of course, some unfortunate person would get the fifty-year-old bachelor.

"I don't know, Horace." Derek scratched his clean-shaven chin. "In this case, you're not choosing the other person. And remember, if you happen to get someone of the opposite gender, there's nothing romantic about being secret pals. We're doing this as friends." He looked at Tonya as if he wanted to make sure she got the point.

She did not appreciate her brother's unspoken message.

"What about a receiver?" Wearing a suit and tie, Reed Dickens looked like a model in a men's fashion magazine.

Derek raised his eyebrows. "A receiver?"

"Like a football receiver." Reed pantomimed catching a football. With those broad shoulders filling out his suit, he was definitely football-player material. "The person is on the receiving end of the encouragement or gifts of the secret pal, so he or she would be called a receiver." He looked around, his green eyes stopping at Tonya.

She smiled at him. *What a gorgeous guy!*

Cheyenne Wilkins, sitting three seats from Tonya, raised her hand. "Derek, the recipient is called a secret pal also."

"But that doesn't make sense." Reed frowned. "I think the recipient should be called a receiver."

Derek shrugged. "It doesn't matter to me, but for the sake of being clear, maybe we should take Reed's suggestion. All in favor?" He waited while a few heads bobbed. "So you'll all be secret pals and receivers." He wrote something down. "Don't forget about our Christmas party on the twenty-third. Everyone needs to come. For the gift exchange, each receiver will get a present from his or her secret pal. So don't put your name on your gift."

A murmur of conversation broke out. Tonya glanced from Reed to Murray Twichell, who was also wearing a suit and tie. He looked at her with his close-set eyes and smiled, showing his straight white teeth.

Returning a faint smile, she looked away. His haircut made him look better than usual, if she must say so herself. But seeing Murray reminded her of his childhood pranks.

Forgive and forget. She sighed. *I'm trying, Lord!*

While Derek answered a few more questions, Tonya glanced over her crimson red fingernail polish and noticed a bump on her left thumb. She drew in a quick breath. A wart? How had she missed that? She would have to make a quick trip to the dermatologist tomorrow.

The Sunday school bell rang, signaling an end to class. As soon as Derek closed in prayer, Tonya stood, determined to talk to Reed.

Cheyenne touched her arm. "Hey, girlfriend! What do you think about the secret pal thing?"

"Oh, I love it!" Tonya looked up into Cheyenne's clear blue eyes. "I can't believe Derek got an idea like that, can you?"

"It wasn't his idea." Cheyenne grinned as she smoothed a strand of blond hair behind her ear. "Callie and I came up with it a couple months ago. I thought he'd completely forgotten about it."

"Evidently you girls made an impression." Tonya leaned toward Cheyenne. "I'm sure that makes *you* happy."

Cheyenne had been in love with Derek since high school. Almost six feet tall, she looked good standing beside Derek, who was six-three. Of course, he had never noticed girls. He was more interested in working on the ranch than going out on a date.

"Well. . ." Cheyenne lowered her voice. "I wouldn't mind being his secret pal."

Tonya giggled. "I'm going to be the best secret pal ever. My receiver guy is going to be the happiest man in the world."

"How do you know it's going to be a guy?"

"Well, I don't, but I'm praying for a certain person." Tonya glanced at Reed. He was deep in conversation with Laurie Smullens, and they were standing awfully close. *No!* She couldn't lose Reed before she even had him. "Excuse me, Cheyenne. I need to talk to someone."

Tonya strode toward Reed like a well-thrown football but was intercepted by Murray Twichell. His aftershave tackled her senses, and she sneezed.

&

Murray took a step back. "Gesundheit."

"Murray!" Tonya's eyes flashed as she sniffed. "You really shouldn't wear such strong aftershave. It's overpowering."

He clenched his jaw. "Sorry. Just wanted to thank you for the great haircut." He'd actually gotten a few compliments, and that had never happened before.

"You're welcome." Her perfectly shaped eyebrows formed a *V* in the middle of her forehead. She stepped to the side of him. "Now if you'll excuse me. . ."

"Don't mean to keep you, Tonya." He gazed into her beautiful dark blue eyes, which were level with his own. Too bad she had such a prickly personality. "I know what an important job you have—playing the piano for the morning church service."

"It *is* important." Her eyes flashed again—like dark lightning.

"I suppose you're right." He felt the tension between them and couldn't keep the sarcasm from his voice. "No one else can play the piano like you."

She planted her hands on her thin hips. "Mrs. Langston is out of town, so we won't have an organist today."

"Ah!" Tilting back his head, he studied her. "So it's just you in all your glory."

She turned her back on him. "Later, Murray."

He watched her stride out of the now-empty room. She sure had a good figure. Amazing how he had never noticed before. Of course he had always wanted to marry Callie, but now that she was married to someone else, Murray was beginning to view Tonya as more than Callie's younger sister. And he liked the view.

As he exited the Sunday school room, a scrap of scripture popped into his mind. *"Man looketh on the outward appearance, but the Lord looketh on the heart."* Tonya's outward appearance was fantastic, but did anyone know the real Tonya? For some reason she brought out the worst in him, and he seemed to bring out the worst in her, too. He wondered what she was really like—in her heart.

It would be intriguing to find out.

❧

Tonya's fingers swept over the piano keys as the parishioners entered the sanctuary. A low buzz of conversation accompanied her playing of "Nothing but the Blood of Jesus." Keeping one eye on her music, she glanced out at the audience every few measures.

Her eyes paused at Reed Dickens. His brown hair was cut perfectly, and Tonya wondered who had styled it. He must have gone somewhere besides Clint's Barbershop. He sat on the back pew—next to Laurie Smullens. Tonya pressed her lips together, determined that Dickens-Smullens would not be a couple for long. *Not if I can help it!*

"No other fount I know. . ." The wavery soprano voice with the slow vibrato could only belong to old Edna Beazer. Her singing got louder as she walked to her spot on the second pew.

Tonya took a deep breath, trying to quell her irritation. Mrs. Beazer used to have a good singing voice, but it had taken a dive with her increasing age. Every Sunday as Tonya played the prelude, however, Mrs. Beazer sang along, loud enough for the entire church to hear. *Amazing that her dentures don't fall out.*

Pastor Reilly strode to the piano, his wrinkled face pale. He leaned toward her and lowered his voice to a stage whisper. "Tonya, we have a problem."

Since she couldn't talk and play at the same time, her fingers stopped. Self-consciously she covered her left thumb with her right hand. She would have to hide that wart until she got rid of it.

She looked up at the pastor's concerned face. "What's wrong?"

"Wayne Holland's wife just called. He's really sick and won't make it. Who can I get to lead the singing?"

"I have no idea." Few of the church members were musical, and Pastor Reilly was completely tone-deaf. She hoped *he* wouldn't have to lead the singing.

The pastor twisted the lapel on his suit coat. "I'll find someone." He dropped his voice. "I have to—we have a visitor this morning."

Tonya watched him walk down the aisle of the crowded

auditorium. She switched to another hymn, hoping Mrs. Beazer wouldn't know this one. Before she started verse two, the pastor came back.

"Okay, we're all set." He rubbed his hands together, seemingly more relaxed. "Do you have a list of hymns for the song leader, Tonya?"

Again she stopped playing. "Who's leading the—"

"So what are we singing?"

Not again. Tonya would recognize that baritone voice anywhere—and the aftershave fragrance that accompanied it. She had to admit that Murray knew music. Every few months he sang a solo in church. Secretly she had always loved his singing voice—and that was the *only* thing she loved about him.

She handed him a service schedule. "Just follow this."

He cracked his knuckles before he took the paper. "Oh, these hymns are easy."

Tonya sighed. Murray needed a lesson in humility.

Five minutes later, he stood behind the pulpit and welcomed everyone to the service.

"Let's all turn to number 496 in your hymnbooks. Number 496." He smiled, exuding confidence. " 'Victory in Jesus.' "

From his chair on the platform, Pastor Reilly leaned forward. "Have the congregation stand, Murray."

"Oh." Murray flashed another smile. "Let's all stand, please."

The audience rustled to their feet as Tonya played a rousing introduction, clipping along at a fast tempo. She ended the intro with a bouncing run up the keys.

Murray looked at her as if he wasn't sure she was finished. She raised her eyebrows and nodded.

"Okay." He lifted his right hand. "All together now on verse one." He waved his hand as he began singing.

Tonya took off at a brisk pace, but by the third measure Murray lagged behind. The people followed him. She slowed down her playing and then—fuming—slowed down some more until the music dragged at a slow tempo.

Only Murray could turn "Victory in Jesus" into a funeral dirge.

At the chorus, she gritted her teeth and sped up the pace, hitting the keys as hard as she could. A few voices in the crowd followed her, while the rest stayed with Murray.

At the end of the first chorus, he stopped the music. "Let's all stay together." He looked pointedly at Tonya. "A little slower on the tempo."

She expelled a hot breath. How slow did they have to go? She played the second verse at a quicker pace than she usually did. Murray glanced at her a few times and she mouthed, "Faster!" At the end of the second chorus, he seated the audience.

What? He wasn't going to sing the third verse?

Murray took a seat on the platform. He set his hymnbook on the little table beside his chair, then looked toward the piano. His eyes narrowed as he glared at her. Now she knew what that phrase *if looks could kill* meant.

❧

"Would you set the table, Tonya?" Mom opened the oven, and the delicious smell of roast beef wafted out.

Tonya knew exactly what she would look like when she was fifty-five years old. Yvette Brandt was still beautiful with her dark blue eyes, perfect facial features, and dark hair, and Tonya looked just like her mother.

Mom straightened up. "We'll have five for Sunday dinner."

"Five? Who's the fifth person?" Since Callie had married Lane Hutchins more than a week ago, the family only included Mom and Dad, Derek, and herself.

Tiny crow's-feet edged her mother's eyes as she smiled. "I invited Murray to eat with us."

"Mom! Did you have to invite *him*?"

Her mother raised her eyebrows. "What's wrong with Murray?"

Tonya opened the silverware drawer more forcefully than

necessary. "I've seen an awful lot of him this weekend." *Awful* being the key word.

"Now don't blame Murray for your speeding ticket." Mom took the roast out of the oven. "Actually, I feel sorry for him. With his father dead and his mom in a nursing home, he's really all alone in the world. He has a lot of responsibility for a young person."

"He's twenty-six. That's not so young."

"Yes it is, Tonya." Mom took the meat platter from the cupboard. "It's too bad he doesn't have any siblings. He must be lonely, living in his parents' house all by himself." She speared the meat and lifted it from the pan. "Some of the women at church are taking turns inviting him for dinner when he's not working on Sunday. Today it's our turn."

Tonya selected five forks from the silverware drawer. How could she argue with Christian charity?

❧

Murray glanced around the large oval dining room table. Jake Brandt, as patriarch of the family, sat at the head with Tonya and Derek seated on his right. On the left, Murray sat beside Mrs. Brandt—Yvette. She insisted he use her first name, but habits were hard to break. He enjoyed eating with other church families, but his favorite place was right here, at the Brandts' table. Passing the food around, he half listened as Jake told about the rare visitor at church that morning.

"He lives up in Canada—Saskatchewan, just over the border from Montana." Jake took a helping of mashed potatoes and passed the dish to Murray. "I invited him for dinner, but he's driving down to Denver this afternoon."

As the conversation flowed around him, Murray took a spoonful of potatoes from the dish and passed it on to Yvette. He was content to eat and listen—and reminisce.

He sat in this very spot one summer as a ten-year-old boy. Callie, who was also ten, sat across the table beside Derek, a year younger. Their twin sisters, Molly and Melissa—whom he could never tell apart—must have been around thirteen, and joined them at the table for warm cookies and milk.

And then there was Tonya, who turned seven years old that July. Her sisters called her *baby sis*, and she was still the spoiled baby of the family.

Murray took a bite of potatoes, glancing up at Tonya as she elaborated about the secret pal idea.

"So I wrote on the card that I was interested in old movies and classical music and that I like the colors blue and purple." She thought for a moment. "I should have put down that I love poetry, too, and also cooking and sewing but—oh well." She raised one shoulder in a slight shrug. "So some guy—or girl—will send me gifts and encouragement, and even pray for me, but that person will remain a secret for six weeks. Isn't that a great idea? I just love surprises."

Murray stopped chewing. *It's all about her.*

Tonya's dark eyes glowed. "I already have some thoughts on what I'm going to do for my secret pal." She turned to her brother. "I'm surprised you thought up that idea, Derek."

He shrugged. "I had a little help."

Tonya giggled. "I know. Cheyenne told me."

Murray popped a piece of roast beef in his mouth. As Tonya continued to dominate the conversation, he thought back to the way she had dominated the song service that morning. Instead of following his lead, Tonya insisted on having her own way, playing the tempo way too fast. It shouldn't be surprising that she'd break the speed limit and then try to argue her way out of a ticket.

He took another bite of meat, savoring the flavor. He had always wanted to belong to this family. Maybe that was why he wanted to marry Callie. But Tonya was the only girl left, so he'd never belong to the Brandt family now. No way would he marry Tonya, no matter how beautiful her face.

three

On Friday evening, Tonya glanced out the living room window. Two headlight beams cut through the darkness, lighting up the snowflakes that floated down to the long driveway. "Mom? Are we expecting company?"

Her mother's voice wafted from the kitchen, along with the aroma of chocolate chip cookies. "Oh, that must be Molly. The nursing home hired a couple extra nurses, so she got the weekend off."

"Really?" A spark of excitement surged through Tonya. "I'll help her with her stuff." She ran to the front closet and pulled on her boots. Grabbing a coat, she threw it on as she sprinted down the snowy steps of the front porch.

Molly parked her car by the door and got out. Long auburn hair flowed over the shoulders of her gray winter coat.

"Molly! Welcome home!"

Her sister looked up. Tiny pricks of the porch light shone in her brown eyes. "Baby sis!"

Tonya hugged her. "You were just here two weeks ago for Callie's wedding. I can't believe you're back so soon. That's a long drive in this weather."

"Yeah, sixty miles on icy, snowy roads. I'm exhausted."

"You do sound tired." Tonya shivered in the cold evening air.

Molly opened the trunk and took out a suitcase. "I'm glad I could get away this weekend. After all, I have my own wedding to plan."

"Oh, Molly, I'm so excited for you." Tonya hugged her again, suitcase and all.

"Thanks. I thought Jonathan would *never* ask me. But when he said he thought it would be nice to get married on Valentine's Day, since it's on a Saturday, I agreed before the words were out of his mouth." Molly giggled. "I think I shocked him."

Tonya took the suitcase from her sister, and they clomped up the front steps together. "You've sure been patient. Haven't you two been going out for five years?"

"Six. At least, it's going to be six years on Valentine's Day." Molly opened the front door. "Our first date was for a Valentine's party at the church in Douglas."

"I didn't know that. So now you've come full circle. Your first date was in the same church where you plan to tie the knot."

"Yep." Molly took off her coat. "And that knot is going to be really tight."

⁂

"How can you plan a wedding in two months?" Tonya sat across from her sister at the dining room table. Both she and Molly flipped through bridal magazines looking at bridesmaid dresses.

"A girl has to do what a girl has to do." Molly grinned. "Of course, I've been thinking about my wedding for years just in case he popped the question. But Jonathan always wanted to wait and get his medical degree first."

"I wonder what changed his mind."

"Callie's wedding. He said when he saw me walk down that aisle as a bridesmaid something hit him."

Tonya smiled. "Must have been one of Cupid's arrows. Callie's wedding was so beautiful, I got hit myself." Her smile faded. "But I have no idea who my groom will be."

Molly reached across the table and patted her hand. "All in good time, baby sis. You have plenty of time."

"No I don't." Tonya pulled her lips into a pout. "I'm twenty-three—practically an old maid."

"So what does that make me? No one else in the family hit twenty-nine before they got married." Molly flipped a page. "That's another reason I jumped at the chance to marry in two months. I want to have six kids, just like Mom."

"At least you had someone to marry all these years." Tonya sighed. "I've had plenty of dates, but no one sticks." She thought of Reed Dickens. "Although I have my eye on someone—a really hot guy. I think he's a doctor, Molly. Wouldn't that be something if we both ended up marrying doctors?"

Molly turned another page. "He and Jonathan will probably talk shop at every family reunion. Hey, here's a pretty dress." She turned the magazine around to show Tonya. "What do you think about this one in pink?"

Tonya gazed at the sleeveless gown. "That would be beautiful and perfect for a Valentine's wedding. But maybe it should be a darker pink or even a fuchsia."

"Good idea—if we can find satin fabric in purplish-red. Do you think we could get fuchsia flowers for the bouquets?"

"Maybe, but that color would look great with a bouquet of light pink roses." Tonya gave the magazine back. "I'm not going to have a winter wedding. I always wanted to get married in June, with pastel dresses for my bridesmaids. Each one will wear a different color."

"Ooh, pastels. I like that. How many bridesmaids will you have? Just the sisters?"

"Plus five or six more. I'd really like ten or twelve girls."

"Ten or twelve?" Molly shook her head. "Really, Tonya—"

"The wedding pictures will be fabulous."

Molly laughed. "Dream on, baby sis."

Tonya sighed. Right now her wedding was nothing *but* a distant dream.

&

Ten minutes later Tonya opened the front door with the sound of the doorbell still reverberating through the house. Callie and Lane stood on the snowy porch.

"Hey!" Tonya pulled Callie into the house with a hug. "When did you guys get back from your honeymoon?"

"Yesterday."

"Yesterday?" Tonya took a step back. She still couldn't get used to Callie without her glasses, which she had worn almost all her life. Her husband, Lane, had paid for laser eye surgery as a wedding gift. "You got back yesterday? Why didn't you call us? Are you staying at Lane's house in Cheyenne?"

"Nope." Callie glanced up at her husband and smiled. "We spent the night at our new house on Little Deer Road."

Tonya didn't miss the look of love that passed between the newlyweds. But before she could even give a wistful sigh, Mom and Molly were there, hugging Callie and Lane. As Callie exclaimed over Molly's new engagement, Dad and Derek joined the group.

"Derek and I are watching an old rerun of *Columbo*." Dad slapped Lane on the shoulder. "Why don't you come on back, Lane? I'm sure the girls will only talk about wedding plans."

"*Columbo* sounds good to me." Lane winked at Callie. "I guess I've spent enough time with my wife this week."

Callie's face tinged pink as she smiled back at him.

The blushing bride. Tonya hoped she would be next.

Soon Tonya joined her sisters and her mom around the kitchen table where they feasted on warm chocolate chip cookies. Callie described the wonders of Yellowstone National Park in the wintertime and the snug cabin they had rented.

Tonya propped her chin in her hand with a wistful sigh. "I can't wait to have my own wedding."

Molly nodded. "Tonya said she's going to have ten or twelve bridesmaids."

Mom raised her eyebrows. "That many, Tonya?"

"Well. . ." She shrugged, not wanting to change her girlhood dreams. "I want to include everyone. Besides, think of how it would look—my husband and I flanked by a dozen girls in beautiful pastel colors. Like a flower garden."

Molly laughed. "That's just like you, baby sis. My three sisters will be enough for me." She picked up the magazine and showed the picture to Mom. "Do you think you could sew three bridesmaid dresses like this in fuchsia for Tonya, Callie, and Melissa?"

Mom studied the picture. "If Tonya helps me, we should have plenty of time to finish them." She picked up her teacup. "But what about your dress, Molly? Are you going to sew it yourself?"

Molly shook her head. "No time. Melissa is going to let me borrow hers. We did some planning last night over the phone."

"Don't you want your own dress?" Tonya couldn't imagine borrowing someone else's bridal gown, even if it was her sister's.

"I love Melissa's dress. We picked it out together, and she doesn't mind sharing."

Mom nodded. "You two always liked the exact same styles."

"That's what happens when you're twins." Callie grinned. "Tonya and I have the opposite tastes in clothes."

"That's for sure." Tonya picked up another cookie. "By the way, Molly, who are we walking down the aisle with?"

Molly counted on her fingers. "Melissa is my matron of honor, and Derek will be the best man."

"Derek?" Mom, Callie, and Tonya said his name in unison.

"What about Jonathan's brother?" Mom took a bite of her cookie.

"He's not coming. It was too hard for him to get away from his mission in India." Molly paused. "I've always wanted to have all my siblings in our wedding, and since Jon's brother couldn't come, he decided on one of my brothers as his best man."

"Why didn't he pick Ryan?" Mom asked. "He's the oldest."

"Jon doesn't know Ryan that well. On the other hand, he and Derek are good friends." Molly resumed her counting. "So, it's Melissa and Derek, Callie and Ryan, and Tonya and Murray."

Tonya's mouth dropped open. "Do you mean Murray Twichell?"

Molly raised her eyebrows. "What other Murray is there? He's Jonathan's cousin, so Jon wants him in the bridal party." She looked concerned. "Is something wrong?"

Tonya dropped her head in her hands. "I cannot get rid of that guy."

Mom placed her arm around Tonya's shoulders. "He gave her a speeding ticket last week, so she's upset with him."

Tonya folded her arms. "Besides that, he's an inch shorter than me, and I know you'll want us girls to wear heels. The pictures will look terrible." Of all the people in Wyoming, she had to get stuck with Murray!

"Jon and I talked about that." Molly rested her chin in her hand. "After all, Jon and my two brothers are all over six feet tall, and Murray is. . .what?"

"Five-six," Callie supplied.

"Right. But Jonathan has a plan." Molly grinned. "His uncle has a pair of elevator shoes from the '70s that he wore in college, and Jon asked if Murray could wear them."

Tonya frowned. "Elevator shoes?"

"I remember those." Mom spread her thumb and index finger about two inches apart. "The entire sole is two to three inches deep, so it makes the man taller. Some people call them platform shoes."

Molly giggled. "Murray will be at least two inches taller than you, baby sis."

"Great!" Tonya rolled her eyes. "Just what I need—Murray looking down his big nose at me during the entire wedding." A sudden thought hit her. "Hey, why don't you make Lane Callie's partner, and then I can walk down the aisle with Ryan?"

Callie shook her head. "Lane is not the groomsman type. He told me that our wedding was the last one he wanted to be in for a while."

"Well, he'll have to be in *mine*." Tonya threw her hands up in the air. "If I'm going to have ten or twelve bridesmaids, I'll need all the guys I can get."

Molly smirked. "Yeah, who knows? You might even have to enlist Murray."

Tonya rolled her eyes. "No way! I can guarantee that Murray Twichell will *never* be in my wedding."

four

On Sunday morning, Tonya's fingers shook as she opened her secret pal envelope. *Please let it be Reed Dickens!* Derek had given each member of the Single Servings an envelope with the 3 x 5 card inside. She furtively glanced around the circle of chairs. Everyone pulled out the card, read it, and tucked it back in the envelope. Cheyenne, who sat next to Tonya, pulled her card up to her face and squinted her eyes, as if the writing was hard to read.

She must have gotten Horace.

"Okay." Derek rubbed his hands together. "Now you know the name of your receiver and what he or she likes. And remember, don't trade cards with anyone." He paused a moment to look at Tonya. "This is the person the Lord wants *you* to encourage." He went on to reiterate his ideas for encouragement, and above all, he admonished everyone to keep it secret.

While he talked, Tonya took a deep breath and pulled her card halfway out. Her shoulders slumped as she read the neat blocky printing. *Murray Twichell. Brown is my favorite color. I enjoy singing, fixing computers as a hobby, and watching football games.* She sighed as she put the card back. *And giving speeding tickets, throwing toads down little girls' shirts. . .*

Cheyenne elbowed her, leaning closer to whisper. "Who'd you get?"

Tonya handed over her envelope. Pulling out the card, Cheyenne peeked at it and raised her eyebrows before giving it back. A moment later Tonya pulled out Cheyenne's card. The writing was so terrible she could barely make out the name.

Reed Dickens.

Tonya's lips parted. Reed went on to describe his favorite things in an entire paragraph of scribbled writing. He *must* be a doctor if his writing was this bad. She held the card close to her face, as Cheyenne had done, and tried to decipher the message.

Reed Dickens. I live in Lusk and work at the hospital as a registered nurse.

Tonya whipped her head toward Cheyenne. "A nurse?" she mouthed.

Cheyenne shrugged. Her attention went back to Derek as he began to teach the Sunday school lesson.

It took another five minutes for Tonya to finish reading the card. Reed not only mentioned his job, but where he had moved from, his favorite foods, his favorite pastimes, his favorite movies, and the name of his ex-girlfriend.

Tonya handed the card back and leaned toward Cheyenne. "That guy is really stuck on himself."

"I'll say," Cheyenne whispered. "No wonder Nicole is his *ex*-girlfriend."

Well, that was one good thing. Tonya still wasn't ready to dismiss Reed as a potential husband. He was too good-looking—*really hot*, that's what he was. And after reading his card about his favorite pastimes, she had an idea. . . .

❧

Murray tried to keep his mind on Derek's lesson, but his eyes kept wandering over to Tonya. He couldn't believe her name was on his card. *From the Lord,* according to Derek. Why did he keep getting stuck with her? His cousin, Jonathan, asked him to be in his wedding, and when Murray agreed, Jon said he would be walking down the aisle with Tonya. Murray could just imagine how she took that news.

However, this secret pal thing might prove to be an interesting situation. At least she would be easy to buy gifts for—old movies, classical music, and the colors blue and purple. He also remembered that she loved poetry, cooking, and sewing.

He watched as Tonya and Cheyenne put their heads together and whispered, showing each other their cards. Murray smirked. So much for keeping their secret pals a secret.

❧

Where is he? Tonya looked out the front window for the fifth time on Monday evening, but no car drove up the long driveway.

Yesterday at church Tonya had invited Reed Dickens to watch the Monday night football game with her family. According to his card, watching the Denver Broncos play football was one of his favorite things. So Tonya invited him to come, made a batch of brownies—her special recipe that the men in her family raved about—and prepared to question him about his life. She had accepted the fact that he was a registered nurse. After all, those female nurses probably needed a strong, buff guy like him to lift the patients.

Now Tonya sat sideways on the sofa so she could look out the window. *Lord, I pray that Reed won't forget about our date.* It would be terrible if he stood her up! She would be so embarrassed. Of course, Dad and Derek would watch the game anyway. *And Lord, I need to pray about my relationship with Reed.* Actually, they had no relationship to speak of, but she hoped this would be "the beginning of a beautiful friendship," to quote Rick in *Casablanca*.

Headlight beams appeared over the hill of the driveway. Tonya jumped up and smoothed her blue and orange Broncos sweatshirt. She was thankful the snow had melted. Opening the door, she ran down the porch steps and out into the cold air but stopped at the same time as the vehicle.

It was a silver SUV, which she recognized as Murray Twichell's new car. The driver's door opened, and Murray stepped out.

Tonya's heart sank down to her tennis shoes. "Murray, what are you doing here?"

He raised his eyebrows as he shrugged. "Is there a law

that I can't drive onto your property? I decided to stop by and help your dad fix his computer. He asked me to come over sometime, and I thought we could watch the Broncos-Raiders game while we worked on it."

"This is not a good night, Murray." She took a step back. He wore that powerful aftershave again, and she didn't want to sneeze. "I'm waiting for my date to show up, and he's going to watch the football game with our family."

"Oh, with the family." Murray's mouth quirked. "Sounds like a hot and heavy social engagement, eh, Tonya?"

She reined in her rising temper. "Would you just leave, Murray? He's going to be here any minute."

He held a palm out toward her. "Okay, I'm leaving." He opened the car door. "By the way, who is this nameless *he*?"

"It's none of your business. Good-bye, Murray." She stomped toward the house. Of all the nerve! Dad had been complaining about his computer for two weeks, and Murray decides to show up tonight.

It didn't help Tonya's mood that Reed was twenty minutes late. The game had started by the time he arrived, but Tonya graciously led him to the den. After exchanging greetings with Dad and Derek, Reed settled on the end of the sofa. Derek was on the other end, and Tonya plopped down between them.

"Wow, what a pass!" Reed perched on the edge of the sofa. "This is going to be a great game."

Derek slipped his arm on the sofa behind Tonya. "Yeah, the Broncos are doing good this year. Ten and four isn't a bad record."

Dad sat back in his recliner. "I doubt if they'll make it to the Super Bowl, though."

Tonya glanced at Reed's handsome profile. Still perched on the sofa's edge, he wasn't paying the least bit of attention to her. She picked up the tray of brownies from the coffee table and held it in front of him, hoping he would notice the artful display. The brownies swirled around in a circle, each one perched on the corner of the next. "Would you like a brownie, Reed?"

She gazed at his brown hair, perfectly styled as usual. His emerald green eyes—such a perfect color to complement his strong facial features—stared at the big-screen TV for a moment before turning to stare at her.

"Uh, what did you say?"

She lifted the tray an inch. "Brownie?"

"No thanks. I'm on a diet. Do you have any popcorn? And something to drink would be nice, too."

Dad motioned to a small table next to his recliner. "We have soda over here, Reed, and a couple empty glasses. Help yourself."

With a small and hopefully undetected sigh, Tonya set the tray down and stood. "I'll microwave some popcorn."

"Light on the butter." Reed rose to get some soda. "And light on the salt, too."

Tonya nodded. "Be right back." She exited to the kitchen.

Mom rinsed a pan in the sink. "How's the game, Tonya?"

She heaved a huge sigh, which had been trying to get out since Reed arrived. "The *game* is fine, but Reed is on a diet, so he wants popcorn."

"We have some." Mom motioned toward the cupboard.

"Do we have any with no taste?" Tonya rolled her eyes. "I wanted Reed to try my special brownies, but now I made them for nothing."

"No you didn't." Mom chuckled as she wiped the counter with her dishrag. "Dad and Derek will polish them off. You'd better get one while you can."

"I don't want a brownie." Tonya pulled a microwavable bag from the popcorn box. "I wanted Reed to try one. He's hardly looked at me since he arrived." She placed the bag in the microwave and pushed a couple of buttons. "All he's talked about so far is the game."

Mom shrugged. "Football's a guy thing. Maybe you can have a nice conversation with him at halftime."

"Maybe." A tiny spark of hope ignited inside. Watching a Broncos game was one of Reed's favorite things to do, so perhaps he would associate good memories with her sitting next to him. It was a start anyway.

She took the big white bowl from the cupboard with the word POPCORN painted in blue cursive. "Do you think I should get individual bowls for the guys?"

Mom shook her head. "They can just grab a handful from the big bowl. Men are not particular when it comes to food."

The popping stopped, and Tonya poured the popcorn into the bowl. When she entered the den, the three men shouted out a cheer of victory.

But the cheer was not for her or the popcorn. All three had their eyes glued to the television, although Dad looked up and smiled at her.

Reed fisted the air. "We have 'em now! The Broncos have it in the bag."

"Here's your popcorn." Tonya made what she hoped was a graceful entrance. She handed the bowl to Reed, making sure the word POPCORN faced him before she took her seat between him and Derek.

Reed took the bowl, his eyes still on the game. "Aww! I can't believe he missed the extra point!"

Derek took a brownie from the tray. "This is only half the game. Even with a twenty-seven-point lead, the Broncos could still lose."

"No way." Reed munched on the popcorn, keeping the bowl between his knees. "The Raiders are playing lousy."

During halftime Reed and Derek talked about stats like they were on a post-game show. Tonya tried to break into the conversation several times, but to no avail.

Finally she leaned a little closer to Reed. "I was a cheerleader for our football team in high school. We had a winning team when I was a senior—state champs."

Reed didn't even look at her as he pointed to the TV. "Hey, this is a great commercial—real creative. Nicole loved it.

She'd always start laughing when it came on."

"Is Nicole your sister?" Dad asked.

Reed pulled his attention away from the screen to look at Dad. "My ex-girlfriend. We once attended a Broncos game in Denver. The game went into overtime, and we won by a field goal. It was cool."

With a sigh, Tonya sat back and folded her arms. It didn't matter how handsome Reed Dickens was—she was ready to cross him off her list as a potential husband.

❧

The rest of the evening only confirmed Tonya's decision. When the score narrowed down to six points between the teams, Reed yelled at each loss and whooped at every gain. But finally Denver lost.

Tonya shrugged. "Win a few, lose a few."

Reed shook his finger at her. "Yeah, but Denver will come back. You'll see." He stood. "Guess I'll be shoving off. Thanks for the invite." He reached over to shake Dad's hand.

Tonya bit her lip. *She* had invited him, not Dad.

"Glad you could come, Reed." Dad smiled, ever the congenial host. "It was good to make your acquaintance."

"Same here." He turned to Derek. "See you on Sunday."

Derek stood. "Actually, I'll see you tomorrow night. We're having the Single Servings Christmas party, remember? The secret pal gift exchange, and all that?"

Reed snapped his fingers. "That's right. Yeah, I'll be there."

"I'll walk you to your car, Reed." Tonya followed him from the room, miffed that he had ignored her all evening. Maybe they could have a decent conversation outside.

But before they even made it to the front door, Reed turned to her. "I think the Broncos lost in the third quarter, don't you? When that long pass was intercepted, it completely turned the game."

She sighed, tired of football. "I'm sure you're right."

"And then when Stokley fumbled the ball. . ." He opened the front door and exited, not even waiting for her.

She slipped outside, closing the door behind her. The cold air smacked her, and she was thankful she was wearing a sweatshirt. "I must admit, I'm not really that big on football."

"Some girls are." He stopped at the door of his car. "Nicole loved it. We could talk football for hours."

I bet. "You never told me much about your family, Reed. Aren't you from Casper?"

"Yeah. Lived there all my life. Nicole is from there, too, but she moved to California—right after we broke up. She moved in with her grandmother."

Forget Nicole, you jerk! "So your parents still live in Casper?"

"Yep. My grandparents settled there after emigrating from England." He grinned. "Did you know that Charles Dickens was my great-great grandfather?"

Tonya's eyes widened. "Wow! That's amazing to be in the direct line of someone so famous."

"Not!" Bending over, Reed actually slapped his knee as he guffawed. "I really pulled one over on you!" He continued chuckling as he pointed at her. "And you believed me!"

Tonya folded her arms. "Very funny, Reed."

"I told Nicole the same thing when we first started dating. She believed me so much she asked my dad about it." He laughed again, big belly laughs, as if it was the funniest thing in the world.

Tonya took a step back, willing to make a quick end of this date. "Thanks for coming. See you tomorrow night at the party." She turned toward the house.

"Uh, yeah. Tomorrow. And thanks, Tonya. I had fun."

She didn't even look back.

five

On Tuesday evening, Murray stepped inside the Sunday school classroom at church, which had been transformed for the Single Servings Christmas party. Like a wagon train, four sofas circled around a large flowered rug that covered the linoleum, and a few wingback chairs were positioned between the sofas. By the door, a tall Christmas tree guarded several presents that peeked out beneath the branches.

Murray scanned the room. Derek, Tonya, and Cheyenne stood at the food table talking. Several other people stood in small groups or sat on the sofas. Everyone held a plate of food.

Shoving his secret pal gift under the tree, Murray removed his jacket, then found an empty hook along the wall already crowded with coats.

"Hey, Twitch!"

Murray grinned. Derek Brandt was the only person who still called him by his old football nickname. Murray still remembered the euphoric feeling of catching a long pass thrown from Derek's arm and running down the field for a touchdown.

Derek motioned to him. "Come over and get some food before we start."

"I'm always game for food." Murray hadn't eaten supper, and he was starving. He nodded a greeting to Cheyenne and Tonya as he picked up a red paper plate decorated with jingle bells.

Derek looked around the room. "Who are we still missing?"

Cheyenne laid her plate on the table. "Corey isn't here yet."

"Neither is Aggie." Tonya nibbled on a cookie. "She told me she might be late."

Murray looked at the array of food, which was mostly in the dessert category. But a tray of small meatballs with a toothpick stuck in each one caught his attention. He grabbed a meatball and popped it into his mouth. "Wow, these are good." He glanced up at Cheyenne. "Who made them?"

"Tonya." Cheyenne smiled, and her dimples creased. "Aren't they wonderful?"

"They really are." Murray looked at Tonya as he placed another meatball on his plate. "Good job, Tonya."

"Thank you." Without smiling, she walked away.

Prickly. Murray took five more meatballs. Why couldn't Tonya be civil to him? He remembered when she had sneezed on Sunday and blamed his aftershave. Maybe she didn't like the smell of his aftershave although he loved the scent. Before attending the party, he had doused himself liberally.

By the time everyone arrived, Murray felt full, having finished his meatballs as well as three brownies and a piece of cake. He chose a comfortable blue chair that he recognized from the Brandts' living room. Some of the other chairs and sofas were from their home, too, and every seat was occupied. Tonya sat on a sofa between Cheyenne and Aggie, who did indeed arrive late, but that didn't keep her from scarfing down the food on her mounded plate. Aggie's hairstyle was tinted green and whipped up like a Christmas tree. Murray leaned forward for a closer look. Little ornaments nestled in her hair, and a tiny gold star crowned the top. Her ears sported huge earrings that resembled Christmas presents.

Presents under the tree. With a shake of his head, Murray sat back.

Derek opened the party in prayer, then Tonya and Cheyenne led the group in a few party games. Murray thought they were childish, but that's how these parties always went. After three games, Tonya and Cheyenne took their seats.

"Thanks, girls." Derek looked relieved that the games were over. "The next thing on the agenda is opening the present from your secret pal."

Corey fisted the air. "Woo! Presents!"

A tittering of laughter followed his outburst.

Derek smiled. "Since Cheyenne works at the post office, I figured she'd be a natural at passing out the packages." He nodded to Cheyenne. "The floor is all yours."

"Thanks, Derek." Cheyenne walked to the Christmas tree and began pulling out the gifts. "By the way, if anyone wants more food, feel free to get some. There's plenty left."

Murray remembered how good the brownies were—chocolate with bits of chocolate chunks and some kind of cream cheese mixture in the center. Approaching the table, he sought out the tray. Only one brownie remained, and he watched in disappointment as Aggie's bejeweled fingers closed around it.

"Oh, Tonya, hon." Aggie bit into it and chewed as she talked. "These brownies are just scrumptious. You'll have to give me the recipe."

Tonya turned from her place on the sofa. "Sorry, it's one of my secret recipes. I made it up myself, and I'm not giving it away." She smiled at Aggie. "But I'm glad you like them."

"Oh, sugar, they're simply delicious." Aggie polished off the brownie and licked two of her fingers.

"They are good, Tonya." Murray nodded to her, hoping she couldn't smell his aftershave from this distance. "Just like the meatballs. You're a good cook."

"Thanks." A little smile curved her lips before she turned back.

Grabbing a cookie, Murray grinned with a feeling of triumph. At least Tonya was thawing out toward him. He took his seat.

Cheyenne stood on the rug in the middle of the wagon train with colorful gifts of various sizes surrounding her feet. She picked up a clipboard from among the packages. "Before you open your present, each receiver must answer a question. If you don't get the answer right, we'll have to skip you until later."

Several groans followed this announcement.

Cheyenne selected a gift and looked at the tag. "This one is for Reed Dickens."

Reed sat next to Laurie Smullens on a love seat, and they seemed rather cozy, in Murray's opinion. Leaning forward, Reed looked confident. "All right. What's my question?"

Cheyenne consulted her clipboard. "This question is from the book *A Christmas Carol* by Charles Dickens. What was the name of Ebenezer Scrooge's employee?"

"Bob Cratchit, of course." Reed sat back with a chuckle. "You have to know your Dickens like the dickens, and that's me." He looked at Laurie and laughed at his own joke. She giggled.

Murray glanced across the room in time to see Tonya roll her eyes.

Cheyenne handed Reed a small rectangular package. He tore off the paper and looked at his gift. "Oh, a Mr. Bean DVD. How cool."

Grabbing another gift, Cheyenne read Corey's name. "Here's your question: What is the translation of Santa Claus?"

Corey frowned. "The translation?"

Cheyenne nodded. "*Santa Claus* is German. What does it mean in English?"

"Who knows?" He shrugged. "Uh, Merry Christmas?"

"Sorry, Corey. We'll have to skip you."

"What?" He raised his hands and dropped them.

Tonya smirked. "The answer is Saint Nicholas. Better luck next time, Corey."

Cheyenne picked up the gift Murray had brought and looked at the tag. "Tonya Brandt."

Trying to present a cool demeanor, Murray glanced at Tonya with nonchalant eyes, but his palms began to sweat.

"Okay, Tonya." Cheyenne looked at her clipboard. "What were the three gifts that the wise men brought to the baby Jesus?"

A beautiful smile lit Tonya's face as she reached for her gift.

"Gold, frankincense, and myrrh."

"That's not fair." Corey folded his arms. "Everyone else gets easy questions."

Murray watched Tonya tear off the bright red and gold Christmas paper he had so meticulously wrapped just an hour ago.

"Ooh, I can't believe it!" She held up the DVD he had purchased. "Twenty old movies from the '40s and '50s. I love it! Thank you, secret pal—whoever you are."

He suppressed a grin as he watched Tonya and Aggie bend their heads together to read the box.

What made Tonya tick? It didn't take much to make her happy. But then again, it didn't take much to make her angry.

An old memory, when Murray and Callie were high school seniors, jumped into his mind. Tonya, a ninth grader, wanted to hang out with them, whining that she didn't have any friends.

"Well. . ." Callie had stuck her hands on her thin hips and stared at Tonya through her thick glasses. "You'd have more friends if you weren't so selfish."

True sibling honesty. Murray watched Tonya and Aggie take the DVDs from the case. Tonya seemed to have some good friends now, but she was still self-centered. On the outside she was beautiful, but what was she really like on the inside? If only he could get to know her—not the Tonya she presented to the world, but the real Tonya deep in her heart.

But how could he do that?

Dating her was out of the question. She'd turn him down flat. Maybe he could correspond with her somehow, but that would only work if she didn't know who he was. She said she loved secrets. He thought about that for a moment, and a plan formed in his mind.

Murray smiled to himself. It just might work, but only if Tonya never discovered his identity.

six

On Christmas morning, Tonya watched her nephews, Peter and Paul, play with the empty boxes on the living room floor. "Why do little kids always like the boxes more than the toys?"

Holly, her sister-in-law, sat cross-legged on the carpet. "Those boxes are big building blocks to one- and two-year-olds." She pushed a strand of brown hair behind her ear. "When our family goes back to Denver, we'll leave the boxes here. Then they'll play with the toys at home."

Tonya gathered up the wrapping paper that had been tossed aside when the family opened their gifts early that morning. Right now Mom, Molly, Melissa, and Callie were in the kitchen preparing Christmas dinner. Dad, Ryan, Jonathan, and Lane, along with Philip, Melissa's husband, had already disappeared into the den to watch the football game.

"I wish Derek were here." Holly stacked her sons' toys in a pile.

Tonya sat down on the blue chair, thankful all their furniture was back in the living room. "You know how community-oriented Derek is. He had to help out at the soup kitchen in downtown Casper." Tonya shook her head. "Personally, I think he should have stayed here with the family, but he decided the Lord wanted him to help the homeless on Christmas day."

"That's very admirable."

"I guess." Tonya leaned her head back and wondered who sat in this chair at the Single Servings Christmas party the other night. A face popped into her mind—a face with a big nose and blue eyes set too close together, framed with reddish-brown hair. Usually she would emit a groan, but she remembered how Murray had complimented her cooking. In that area, he was a lot nicer than Reed Dickens. Murray was probably spending a quiet day with his mom at the nursing home in Douglas. With all the siblings Tonya had, she couldn't imagine what a quiet Christmas would be like.

"Tonya?" Callie called from the dining room. "Come help me set the table."

Tonya rose and made her way to the dining table. "How many are we having for dinner?" She glanced at herself in the mirror above the fireplace mantel as she walked by. Holly and Callie hadn't even bothered to put on makeup this morning, but Tonya paused to make sure hers still looked good.

"We have thirteen people, but only ten will fit around the table." Callie set the silverware box on the sideboard and opened it. "Mom said we could stick Peter and Paul at the little card table with one of the adults."

Holly walked into the dining room. "I'll sit with them."

Tonya looked at her sister-in-law, who never seemed to have a moment to herself. "I'll sit with the boys, Holly. You sit with Ryan and the rest of the family."

"Are you sure, Tonya? You don't know what you're getting into. They need a lot of help."

"It will be good experience for the future."

"If you're sure." Holly smiled. "It will be nice to eat a quiet dinner for once."

Tonya smiled back. "Hey, I can handle this. Besides, Peter and Paul and I are the only single people here today, so we'll sit at the singles' table."

An hour later, after cutting up Peter's turkey into small pieces, stopping Paul from throwing his sippy cup at her, and wiping mashed potatoes off both boys' fingers, Tonya wished she could eat her dinner at the other table. She still had mashed potatoes in her hair where Paul grabbed it. That must look real good—white clumps of potatoes in her dark hair. She should run upstairs after dinner and wash it.

Wiping the scalloped corn from Peter's face, she listened to the conversation and laughter from the big table, wishing she could join in. She sighed. Everyone here, all twelve of them, had a partner. Even her two little nephews had each other. But Tonya was the thirteenth person, the unlucky one...the lonely one.

Lord, I want a man!

The doorbell rang, and the room quieted.

Dad placed his napkin on the table as he stood. "Now who could that be?"

"It must be someone we know, Dad." Tonya popped a forkful of mashed potatoes into her mouth. Living out in the country, the Brandts didn't get many visitors.

Dad left the dining room. "It's probably someone from the church wishing our family a merry Christmas."

The conversation picked up again as Tonya wiped Paul's hands for the third time.

A few minutes later Dad came back, carrying a long thin box. "Well, well. We have a special delivery for Miss Tonya Brandt."

She looked up. "For me?"

Dad grinned. "Is your name Tonya Brandt?"

"It sure is." She jumped up as a thrill buzzed through her.

The family crowded around as she took the long box from Dad and sat on the blue chair in the living room.

"Must be a rifle," Ryan quipped.

Tonya opened the lid and gasped, staring at a mass of long-stemmed red roses. Her sisters broke out in exclamations.

Mom placed her hand around Tonya's shoulders and gave her a squeeze. "A dozen red roses, Tonya. And there's a card." She pointed at the envelope nestled among the stems.

Tonya picked it up. *Miss Tonya Brandt* was scripted in beautiful penmanship on the outside of the envelope. She pulled out an old-fashioned Christmas card—a Currier and Ives engraving of a couple ice-skating on a pond. Inside a preprinted message wished her a happy holiday, and then the sender wrote in his perfect penmanship, *Merry Christmas from Your Secret Admirer.*

"Well, who is it, Tonya?" Dad asked.

She glanced around at the curious faces. "It's from a secret admirer!"

This announcement precipitated a cloudburst of conversation. When the speculations died down, the men of the family exited to the dining room, but her sisters and mom stayed to discuss the situation.

Tonya couldn't keep the smile from her face. "Wow, I can't imagine who sent this."

Molly tossed her hair over her shoulder. "Do you think it's that doctor you told me about?"

"Reed? No way. He has terrible handwriting. Besides, he's not interested in me." *And the feeling is mutual.*

"On the other hand. . ." Callie pointed toward the signature with a stick of celery. "Maybe that's not his handwriting. He could have had the salesgirl at the florist sign the card."

Mom nodded. "You wouldn't think a man would have such beautiful penmanship."

Melissa leaned over and picked up the box's lid, which had fallen to the floor. "It was sent from Blooms and Buds Florist, Douglas, Wyoming."

Callie sat down on the ottoman. "That's where we all got our wedding flowers since Fort Lob doesn't have a florist. That's the closest one."

Melissa knit her brows together. "No clues there."

"Who cares who sent them?" Joy bubbled up inside Tonya, but she didn't want to act like a desperate teenager. "This is probably a one-time thing. Most likely I'll never hear from him again."

"But what a nice surprise for you." Mom gave Tonya a quick kiss on her forehead before turning back to the dining room. "Let's get dessert on the table, girls. Tonya, you need to put those roses in water."

Tonya was the last to leave the living room. "Thank you, Lord," she whispered. So what if this was a one-time thing? She would always be thankful for it. Carrying the box out to the kitchen, a feeling of peace enveloped her.

Later, as she helped her sisters finish the dishes, the doorbell rang again. Tonya ran to answer it. A uniformed deliveryman stood on the porch, holding a square box in one hand, a clipboard and pen in the other.

He raised his eyebrows. "Tonya Brandt?"

"Yes, that's me."

He thrust the clipboard toward her. "Sign on the next line, please."

Tonya's hand shook as she wrote her name, then exchanged the clipboard for the package. "Thank you."

With a smile, she brushed back her hair, and her fingers ran into something gooey. Oh great—she had forgotten about the mashed potatoes. *How embarrassing.*

The man grinned, gazing at her face a moment before he turned back to his truck. Tonya closed the door, annoyed that her looks were not perfect. She would have gone upstairs to wash her hair right then if not for receiving a second mysterious gift.

Again she took a seat on the blue chair, and again the family crowded around her. This time her secret admirer had sent a huge box of chocolates.

"Hey, candy!" Ryan grabbed the box. "You're gonna share, aren't you, sis?"

"Help yourself." She felt generous, even though the candy might be gone by the time the men got finished with it.

An envelope lay at the bottom of the package with that same beautiful penmanship. This time it said, *For Tonya.*

"Ooh." Molly winked at her. "He's getting more intimate."

Tonya held her breath as she opened the envelope. The card had a winter scene with an old-fashioned Victorian house decorated for Christmas. The inside was blank, except for what was written in flowing cursive: *Sweets for the Sweet. May you have a blessed Christmas, Tonya. Your Secret Admirer.*

"Wow, two gifts on Christmas Day." Callie dug her cell phone from her purse. "I have to call Cheyenne. She's not going to believe this."

Tonya giggled. "I'll call Aggie. She always told me if I wait, I'll find my man."

"Sounds like he found you." Melissa cocked an eyebrow.

Tonya breathed out a happy sigh. God had sent her a man, even if he was only temporary.

seven

Early Friday morning Murray entered the Trailblazer Café. Usually the restaurant bustled with breakfast customers, but today only two couples, the Whitneys and the Pipers, sat in booths by the large windows that looked out on Main Street. Bruce MacKinnon was the sole customer sitting at the long counter.

Murray took the seat next to Bruce. "Morning, Bruce." He laid his patrol hat on the empty stool beside him. "I'm surprised you're not eating at a table full of your old cronies." He grinned at the dignified Scotsman.

Bruce shrugged. "It's the day after Christmas." His *r*'s rolled slightly with his brogue. "Everyone is still celebrating with their families, but my son and his family left for Salt Lake City early this morning." He glanced at Murray's patrolman uniform. "I see there's no more holiday for you."

"Nope, it's back to work. Someone has to keep law and order in this sleepy town."

"Aye." With a smile, Bruce set his coffee cup on the saucer. "There's so much crime in Fort Lob. Who knows? You might catch a madman speeding down Main Street."

"Hey, you're right." Murray glanced at his watch. "It's 7:18. I need to be sitting in my patrol car at 8:45, just in case Tonya Brandt decides to break the sound barrier." He laughed, thinking of the expensive gifts he had sent her yesterday. He had paid almost double to get them delivered on Christmas Day.

"Say, speaking of Tonya. . ." Bruce lowered his voice. "I heard she has a secret admirer."

Murray raised his eyebrows. "No joking?" *That didn't take long.* "Where'd you hear that from?"

"Agatha Collingsworth called me last night. Word is that Tonya received a couple packages yesterday from some man who is admiring her from a distance." Bruce chuckled. "The poor boy is probably too scared to ask her out for a date."

Murray hadn't thought how others would perceive his actions. "Well, she's so pretty. You have to give the guy credit for trying."

Coffeepot in hand, Joyce Hediger approached Murray from the other side of the counter. Her ample white waitress uniform already had stains on it. "Are you discussing Tonya Brandt's secret admirer? Isn't that a hoot?" She gave a toothy smile as she poured Murray a cup of coffee.

If Joyce knew about it, the whole town must know. "Where did you hear it, Joyce?"

"Barb Lathrop told me. She heard it from Cheyenne Wilkins. Sounds like Tonya was on cloud nine last night."

So Tonya was excited. Murray tried not to smile too broadly. "I suppose nothing like that ever happened to her before."

Joyce laughed as she took three little creamers from her pocket and set them beside Murray's cup. "Tonya has so many boyfriends, this guy is just one of the many. I bet she's adding him to her list. She always liked attention, you know."

Murray's initial happiness faded.

Joyce set the coffeepot on the counter. "The usual, Murray? Scrambled eggs with toast?"

"Sure." He watched Joyce waddle away before he turned to Bruce. "Does, uh, Tonya know who her secret admirer is?" He dumped a creamer into his cup.

Bruce shook his head. "Not that I'm aware. Agatha didn't say."

Murray stirred his coffee. He couldn't ask too many questions or people would get suspicious. But now he *definitely* didn't want Tonya—or anyone else for that matter—to discover his identity. Bruce thought he was too scared to ask her out, and Joyce thought Tonya didn't care who he was.

Of course, Bruce was right. Murray was afraid to ask Tonya out. But then, his purpose was to find out what she was really like. There was an end to his means, and Murray intended to see it through.

He was glad the post office was open today.

❧

The phone rang at The Beauty Spot on Saturday morning, just as Tonya finished sweeping up from the last haircut. Aggie was at the other beauty station, giving Gloria Schutzenhofer a perm.

"I'll get the phone, Aggie." Tonya walked to the cash register and plucked the receiver from the wall phone after the third ring. "The Beauty Spot, this is Tonya."

"Hi, girlfriend!" Cheyenne's voice came over the line. "You're just the person I want to talk to. Your secret admirer has been busy and, let me tell you—that guy gets around. I have a slew of letters here at the post office for you."

Tonya's heart leaped into her throat. "Really?"

"They're all addressed to Miss Tonya Brandt." Cheyenne chuckled. "For a man, he sure has beautiful handwriting."

"Wow, this is so exciting!"

"What's going on, hon?" Aggie called from her station.

Tonya held up a *one moment* finger to Aggie. "How many are there, Cheyenne?"

"Let's see. . . . There's two letters postmarked from Lusk, three from Douglas, one from Cheyenne, and two that were mailed here in Fort Lob."

Tonya counted silently. "Eight letters! I can't believe it."

"Believe it, girl. Do you want Bernie to deliver them to your house with the rest of the mail, or do you want to swing by the P.O. and pick them up?"

"I'll be there in five minutes!" She laughed. "Thanks, Cheyenne."

Hanging up the phone, Tonya turned to Aggie and Gloria. "My secret admirer sent me eight letters in the mail!" She pulled her purse from under the counter. "I'm going to run to the post office and get them, Aggie. Is that okay?" She grabbed her coat from the hook near the door.

"Only if you let me read them, too." Aggie cackled out a laugh. "This will fuel the town gossip for weeks to come, and we'll do our part. Right, Gloria?"

Gloria's thin eyebrows formed a *V* in the middle of her forehead. "I never gossip."

Tonya turned away so Gloria wouldn't see her laughing. That woman was such a gossip that some people called her *Gloria the Grapevine*.

Pushing open the door, Tonya walked out into the chilly December weather. An inch of snow covered the ground. But even if the weather were warm, she wouldn't walk the three blocks to the post office. She climbed into her red Hyundai and started the engine.

Maybe, after she read these eight letters, she could figure out this guy's identity.

๛

On Monday Murray sat in his SUV at police headquarters in Cheyenne, Wyoming. He'd been off duty for fifteen minutes, but he wanted to stay in the city to mail a few cards to Tonya. The clipboard rested on his steering wheel, and he tapped a pen thoughtfully against his lips.

He read over the words he had written on a piece of notebook paper.

In the winter of my discontent,
Your beautiful face rivals the brilliance of the sun,
The beauty of roses at their peak. . . .

"Nah." He crossed out some of the words and rewrote the poem.

In the winter of my discontent,
Your face brightens my day like a multihued rainbow,
Rivaling the brilliance of the sun,
And the beauty of a rose garden at summer's peak.

He sat back and read over the revision. "That stinks."

Crumpling the paper, he threw it with the other wadded

papers on the passenger's seat. "Okay, I'll take one more stab at it." He thought a few minutes before writing. Maybe he would send this one to Tonya.

He wrote carefully, making sure his penmanship was perfect. In seventh grade he had won an award for best handwriting in the entire school, and he had been proud of his ability—until a couple of ninth-grade boys laughed at him and called him a sissy. He never wrote in cursive again.

In the winter of my discontent,
One look at your beautiful face,
Like a beam of brilliant sunshine in a dark place,
Lifts my countenance, warming my entire being.

"Hmmm. . ." Was this any good? Well, no matter. He would send it anyway. After all, Tonya liked poetry. Tomorrow he would visit the library and check out some of the classics—some of the poets he loved himself. Maybe he'd copy something by Henry Longfellow or Lord Tennyson. He snapped his fingers as a name hit him. *Elizabeth Barrett Browning!* Perfect.

Now it was on to the jewelry store.

❧

That week Tonya made a run to the post office every day during her lunch hour. And every day at least four letters from her secret admirer waited for her. But as she entered the post office on Wednesday, she frowned, chewing on her bottom lip. She wasn't any closer to guessing who this man was than she had been on Christmas Day.

Tonya waited in line while Mrs. Hochstetler bought a book of stamps at the counter.

"I just don't know which ones to buy." Mrs. Hochstetler's white hair quivered slightly as she looked over the selection of stamps that Cheyenne held in front of her. "I liked the Christmas stamps this year. I can't believe it's already New Year's Eve. Another year begins tomorrow."

"Time flies." Cheyenne smiled. "Are you going to stay up until midnight to bring in the New Year?"

"Oh, I can't stay awake that late." Mrs. Hochstetler gave a

little laugh. "I'll be in bed at nine o'clock."

While Cheyenne was busy helping the elderly woman decide which stamps to purchase, Murray Twichell walked through the door. A gun holster rested at the right hip of his uniform.

"Hi." He nodded at Tonya, stopped at the row of post office boxes, and thrust a key in one of them.

Mrs. Hochstetler finally settled on the stamps. She toddled outside, wishing Cheyenne and Tonya a happy New Year. The door closed behind her.

"Tonya, guess what?" Cheyenne pulled a box from beneath the counter. "You have a package today."

"A package!" Tonya almost squealed. Even though everyone in town knew about her secret admirer, she was glad no one else waited in line at the post office. Murray was the only other person in the building. "Is it from *him*?"

"I don't know—there's no return address." Cheyenne laughed as she pushed a small priority mail box toward her. "But that's his handwriting." She pointed to Tonya's name in perfect cursive on the label.

Tonya bit her lip as she opened it and pulled out a small black cardboard box. The words RED MESA JEWELRY CO. were embossed in gold letters on the top. She sucked in a breath. "He bought me jewelry."

"Wow." Cheyenne leaned forward, her arms folded on the counter. "I never heard of the Red Mesa Jewelry Company before." She picked up the mailing box and looked at the postmark. "Fort Collins, Colorado. Your secret admirer sure likes to travel."

"This is so exciting." Tonya was about to lift the lid from the box when she felt someone beside her. She glanced to her right.

Murray peered at the jewelry box before meeting her eyes. "Sorry to interrupt, but it looks like you might be here awhile." He spoke to Cheyenne. "I need to buy a book of stamps."

"Okay." Cheyenne opened a drawer. "We have flag stamps, forever stamps—"

"Flags are good." Murray pulled his wallet from his back pocket.

Tonya didn't wait for their transaction. Opening the box, she gazed at the jewelry case covered in black velvet and raised the hinged lid. A pendant necklace reposed on creamy silk. The chain disappeared underneath, but silver scrollwork held a blue stone.

"Oh. . ." She breathed out a wondrous sigh as she lifted the necklace from the box. "This is beautiful."

Cheyenne handed Murray some change. "Let's see it, girlfriend."

Tonya held it out for her inspection.

"Tonya! This must be a real sapphire." Cheyenne held it close to her face. "At least it looks real to me."

"Let me see it." Murray took the necklace and studied it a moment. "Yep. Definitely real. Of course, you wouldn't expect your boyfriend to give you some fake rhinestone." He grinned as he handed it back.

Normally Murray's comment would aggravate her, but Tonya was too happy to be bothered by him today. "I want to wear this." She took off her coat and laid it on the counter. Brushing her hair out of the way, she pulled the pendant up to her neck and tried to fasten the clasp in the back but couldn't feel the hook. She turned her back to Murray. "Fasten this for me."

"Oh, uh, sure."

Out of the corner of her eye, she saw him lay his stamps and a set of keys on the counter. Then she felt his fingers behind her neck. It took a little longer than she thought it should, but she stood still while he worked on it.

"Okay, there you go." Murray picked up his keys and stamps.

"Thanks." Tonya turned toward Cheyenne. "What do you think?"

"Looks great." Cheyenne leaned her chin in the palm of her hand and gave a wistful sigh. "I wish a certain someone would become *my* secret admirer."

Tonya shook her head. "I'm afraid my brother doesn't have a romantic bone in his body. He would never think of sending you cards and jewelry." She sighed. "I sure wish I knew who sent me this. I can't believe the money he's spent. This sapphire must have cost him a bundle."

"Don't forget postage. He's going through stamps like crazy."

Murray pivoted and walked out the door. "Have a good day, ladies."

"Happy New Year, Murray." Cheyenne stood up straight. "I'm glad tomorrow is New Year's Day. I can sleep in."

"But the post office will be closed, and I won't get any mail from my secret admirer." Tonya fingered the necklace.

Cheyenne reached under the counter and pulled out a small stack of envelopes. "You have mail today. Five letters."

"Wow." Tonya smiled as she took them. "Would you believe he wrote a poem for me? He's so sweet. I'm saving all the cards, and it's quite a collection. I wish I could thank him."

Cheyenne grinned. "I have a feeling you'll find out who he is—eventually."

❧

Murray glanced at the clock above his desk. Nine o'clock on New Year's Eve. Just enough time to write a few cards to Tonya before he had to go to work tonight. He sighed, not relishing all the arrests he'd probably have to make in the early morning hours or the drunken parties he might have to crash.

He creased down the page of the library book and carefully copied the poem on a piece of notebook paper. He had selected "How Do I Love Thee? Let Me Count the Ways" by Elizabeth Barrett Browning. It certainly had a better cadence than his poor attempts at poetry, and the subject matter seemed appropriate, even though he didn't love Tonya.

But. . .what if that happened? What if they fell in love?

His lips curved into a smile as he thought back to her little squeal at the post office. He had waited for her daily visit, hanging out at Gilman's Pharmacy across the street and then entering the post office after she did. Her reaction was more than he had hoped for. He couldn't believe she asked him to hook the necklace clasp. Fastening a necklace was something husbands did for their wives, and it gave him a strange feeling.

Her skin was so soft.

Sitting back, he recalled the girls' conversation about the amount of money he had spent. *I guess I am spending a lot on her.* But what else did he have to spend his salary on? Medicare paid for Mom's nursing home bill, and the house had been paid off years ago. Actually, buying expensive gifts for Tonya was fun.

Picking up the library book, he went back to "How Do I Love Thee." When he finished, he folded the paper and placed it inside the card. Too bad the post office would be closed tomorrow. He read through the preprinted poem that started, "I thought of you today." His eyes traveled to the words he had penned at the bottom of the card, and he smiled to himself.

Tonya would be surprised.

eight

On Friday afternoon, January second, Tonya stared at Cheyenne as she stood in the post office. "Only one card?" Since the post office was closed yesterday, Tonya thought a dozen envelopes would be waiting for her today.

Her friend shrugged. "Sorry. That's it."

Tonya had decided to pick up her mail after work, and now several people queued behind her. She turned and left the building. Walking out into the chilly parking lot, she glanced across the street. Murray Twichell strode toward the Cattlemen's Diner. He gave her a little salute before entering the restaurant.

Tonya waved back. Murray was going to the diner for supper. When he wasn't traveling through the state for the Wyoming highway patrol, he always ate there.

She stopped beside her car. *Hmmm. . .he travels a lot.* Her eyes widened, but almost in the same second, she dismissed the thought. Her secret admirer couldn't be Murray—of all people. He had never even liked her. Besides, he wrote in blocky printing. At least, that's how he wrote her speeding ticket.

She sighed. *Precious memories, how they linger.*

Opening the car door, she laid the card on the passenger seat. She would savor it when she got home. But what if her secret admirer was tired of sending letters to her? Or perhaps he had lost interest, and this would be his last one.

Or maybe he's running out of money.

Well, it was fun while it lasted. Starting the engine, she looked down at the lone envelope on the passenger's seat.

It couldn't be the last one!

Grabbing the envelope, she tore it open and pulled out the

59

card. A piece of paper fell into her lap, and she unfolded it. Her eyes traveled across the poem in his perfect handwriting.

How do I love thee? Let me count the ways.

I love thee to the depth and breadth and height

My soul can reach. . . .

Tonya gave a wistful sigh as she read on. Her secret admirer loved her! He wasn't ending their relationship.

She looked at the front of the card—a Norman Rockwell reprint of a cozy couple. *He's so romantic.* She read the poem on the inside and then read what he wrote at the bottom. Jerking upright, she gasped. "I can't believe it!"

Throwing the gears into DRIVE, she peeled out of the parking lot and roared down Main Street.

❧

"Mom, I'm home!" Tonya raced up the stairs and entered her bedroom. Her computer waited on the desk by the window. She paced the room while it booted up.

Mom appeared at the doorway. "Tonya, what's going on? I've never seen you in such a hurry."

"Read this." Picking up the card, she pointed to his handwriting at the bottom.

Mom's dark blue eyes shifted from left to right over the words. "Oh, he gave you his e-mail address."

Tonya grinned. "Now I can write to him. And he calls himself Poetry Lover Guy. Isn't that funny? His e-mail address is poetryloverguy@sweetmail.com." She picked up the poem. "And look at this. He copied a poem by Elizabeth Barrett Browning."

Mom glanced at it. " 'How Do I Love Thee? Let Me Count the Ways.' That's very famous."

"What's really cool is that Elizabeth Barrett and Robert Browning corresponded with each other, and when they finally met, Robert asked her to marry him." Tonya plopped down on her desk chair. "I hope that happens with this guy and me."

"Now, Tonya. . ." Mom took a seat on the bed. "You need

to be careful. It's one thing to have a secret admirer, but quite another thing to correspond over the Internet with a stranger. A lot of young women have gotten into dangerous situations doing that very thing."

"I know." Tonya eyed her mother. "I won't do anything foolish. Do you think I'm going to run away and meet him somewhere by myself?"

"I certainly hope not."

"Here's the plan." Tonya giggled, feeling a bubble of excitement. "I'm going to invite him over for dinner with the family. After all, he can't keep his identity a secret forever. Then you can meet him at the same time and judge him for yourself."

Mom stood. "Please wait a couple weeks before you ask him for dinner. Let's see what he says on the e-mail first."

Tonya gave an exasperated sigh. "Oh all right. I'll wait."

"Good." Mom started toward the door. "Supper will be ready in twenty minutes."

Tonya opened her e-mail program. "I'm going to write and thank him for all the cards he sent me." She clicked on the New tab.

"Don't forget the roses, candy, and sapphire necklace." Mom's voice faded down the stairway.

"How could I?" Tonya fingered the necklace she'd worn for the past two days. She paused to think before she began typing.

Dear Poetry Lover Guy. . .

੭

The front door to Murray's house squeaked open as he turned the key in the lock. Walking into the living room, he glanced at the computer sitting on the desk in the corner. It wouldn't surprise him if Tonya had already written him.

But he would wait.

He trudged up the creaky wooden stairs to his bedroom. He had been on patrol for two straight days, since New Year's Eve, and he wanted to get out of his uniform, take a shower, and don a pair of jeans and a T-shirt. Amazingly, he had both Saturday and Sunday off. That seldom happened, and the thought of who might invite him over for Sunday dinner drifted through his mind.

But right now he was tired. The New Year festivities had taken their toll while he helped keep law and order on the streets of Cheyenne. Tonight he would relax, microwave a bag of popcorn, and dig out one of Mom's old romantic movies to watch.

His thoughts jumped to Tonya. Sitting by a window at the Cattlemen's Diner, he watched her tear out of the post office parking lot. It almost made him angry. But her irresponsible driving was most likely his fault. She had read his card and wanted to e-mail him. He shook his head. That girl was so impulsive, so unlike him in every way.

Opposites attract.

That's what his mom always told him. Mom was a quiet, demure Irish woman in her thirties when she met Anson Twichell—a loud, outgoing lawyer and the life of every party. Murray grinned, remembering how jolly Dad could be. He lived life to the full—until the day it was cut short by a heart attack. Murray had been fourteen.

He wished for the millionth time his father was still living.

Walking downstairs, Murray booted up the computer and clicked on his e-mail. Sure enough, an e-mail from Tonya Brandt waited for him. A spark of curiosity flew through him, and he leaned forward.

Dear Poetry Lover Guy,

Thank you so much for all the cards you've sent me, as well as the roses, candy, and the sapphire necklace. I wear the necklace every day—it's beautiful, and I love it! The cards have been wonderful. I love receiving mail from you, and I'm so glad you gave me your e-mail address so I could write back and thank you.

Who are you? Tell me all about yourself. Do I know

*you? Do you go to our church? Are you a resident of
Fort Lob, or do you live in Lusk or Cheyenne? What
do you do for a living? How old are you? Nothing like
this has ever happened to me before, and I really want
to meet you.*

> *Please reply, and thanks again.*
> *Love ya, Tonya.*

Murray read the letter once more. She certainly asked a
lot of questions—most of which he wouldn't answer. As for
meeting him, she would be waiting into eternity if he had
his way.

≈

"I hope he wrote back." On Saturday morning, Tonya tapped
her fingernails on the desk, waiting for her e-mail to load.
She didn't have to work today. Saturday was usually the
busiest day at The Beauty Spot, but Aggie had hired a new
beautician, Connie, who would help handle the customers
this weekend.

Tonya had checked her e-mail several times last night, but
there was nothing. Now as her inbox opened, a post from
Poetry Lover Guy appeared.

Her heart gave a leap, and she clicked it open.

Hi Tonya,
    *I'm glad you enjoyed all the letters and gifts I sent. It
was fun to send them to someone so beautiful. But admiring
you from a distance is one thing. I thought it would be better
if we could correspond with each other. I want to get to
know you.*

An arrow of fear pierced her heart. Could Mom be right?
Was this a stranger with evil motives? Some Internet fiend?

Tonya took a deep breath. *Calm down, girl.* After all, he
couldn't reach out of the monitor and grab her by the throat.
She continued reading.

I'll answer some of your questions. Who am I? Well, let's just say I'm a guy who likes poetry and old movies. Where do I live? Somewhere in Wyoming. How old am I? Hmm...between the ages of eighteen and eighty-eight.

Tonya huffed out a breath. He wasn't answering her questions at all! She read the next line.

I watched Singing in the Rain *last night. Great movie!*

Tonya's irritation melted. That movie was one of her favorites, too.

The rest of the letter talked about five other old movies he loved. Tonya grinned. She had seen them all and couldn't wait to discuss them with him. At the bottom, he signed off.

Your secret admirer,
Poetry Lover Guy
P.S. My friends call me "Poe" for short.

Tonya laughed out loud. *Poe?* What kind of name was that? But she had to admit it was better than calling him *Poetry Lover Guy* or *Mr. Guy.*

If only she knew his real name.

๏

The days flew by for Murray. Every evening an e-mail waited for him from Tonya, and every evening he replied—unless he had to work. Some nights he couldn't get on a computer, especially when he was out in the boondocks in the middle of Wyoming.

Tonya wrote lengthy letters, but it was all surface talk about her job, her family, her friends. He was not getting to know the real Tonya at all, which had been his objective.

One Thursday evening, Murray grabbed a can of cola and settled in front of his computer. Since he was off work that day, he'd had plenty of time to think about their relationship.

If he took a risk and revealed his heart, perhaps she would do the same.

Dear Tonya,

After three paragraphs of the usual chatter, he delved into exposing his heart.

I live by myself in a big old house, and tonight I stood by the window for a half hour watching the snowflakes drift down. I'm an introspective person and ponder a lot about my life. Sometimes loneliness overwhelms me. I'm corresponding with you—I must admit—for my own sake as well as for yours. I look forward to reading your e-mails every evening. Reading about your life and sharing things about mine causes the loneliness to disappear.

He read over the lines. Was he revealing his heart too much or not enough? He thought of his birthday coming up next Monday on January twenty-sixth. Would anyone remember it? Did anyone even know?

Sure, his mom would remember, and he would visit her in the nursing home that day. But even though he loved his mom, a quiet visit with her wasn't the way he wanted to celebrate his birthday. What he really wanted to do was to ask Tonya out— not as "Poe," but as Murray. If only he could take her to a nice restaurant to celebrate, then he wouldn't have to eat alone.

Stifling a sigh, he continued typing.

Thanks, Tonya, for writing to me. You make my day with every letter. Ever yours, Poe.

He hit the SEND button before he lost his nerve and deleted the whole thing.

Sitting at the desk, he took a few moments to pray, which made him feel better. He wasn't really alone. The Lord knew what was going on in his life, and He had a plan. Murray would just have to wait for it.

He stood and stretched. Time for another old movie.

❧

Tears formed in Tonya's eyes. Poe sounded so sad. In the back of her mind the thought niggled that perhaps this guy *was* a predator, trying to pluck at her heartstrings with his talk of loneliness. The next step would be for him to invite her to meet him in some dark alley.

She grimaced.

On the other hand, two could play this game. With a determined mind-set, she began typing.

A few minutes later, Mom entered the room. "Are you still at the computer, Tonya?"

"I'm writing a letter to Poe."

"I figured that." Mom stood behind Tonya as she continued typing. "What does LOL mean?"

Tonya grinned. "You're so computer illiterate, Mom. It's an abbreviation that means 'laughing out loud' or, as some people say, 'lots of laughs.' You write it at the end of a sentence when you're joking. Or you could write JK instead. That means 'just kidding.'"

"Oh." Mom nodded. "Kind of like the old 'ha!' that Grandma writes in her letters."

"Exactly." The keyboard buttons clicked as Tonya continued her sentence.

Mom leaned over her. "What does BTW mean?"

"By the way." Tonya stopped typing. She had written her opening comments to Poe and wanted to say something more personal, but she didn't want her mother to read it. "Do you mind, Mom? I can't concentrate when you're reading over my shoulder."

"I was on my way to bed." Mom bent to kiss her daughter's forehead. "It's almost eleven, and you have to get up early for work tomorrow morning."

"I know. And don't worry, I won't be up late. Since it's

been snowing, I plan to get up a half hour earlier tomorrow morning and take my time driving to work. I sure don't want Murray to give me a ticket."

"Good for you." Mom walked to the door. "Good night."

"Night, Mom." Tonya turned back to the computer, ready to pour out her heart to Poetry Lover Guy.

nine

On Friday morning, Tonya watched Crystal Larsen walk out of The Beauty Spot, sporting her new hair color. The blond highlights looked great on Crystal, and Tonya silently congratulated herself on her good fashion advice.

"This morning's been so busy." With a broom, Aggie swept hair into a dustpan. "But I'm glad. Seems like we have more customers when the snow stops." She leaned on the broom handle. "You sure have been quiet today, Tonya."

"I've been thinking about Poe."

"Who else?" Aggie laughed. "The whole town knows about that secret admirer of yours. So, what did he write last night?"

"I feel so sorry for him. He's lonely."

"Aren't we all?" Aggie plopped down in the beautician chair, and her brown eyes turned serious. "You know who really helps curb my loneliness?" She glanced toward the door, as if checking to make sure no customers were entering.

Aggie, lonely? Tonya raised her eyebrows. "Who?"

"Bruce MacKinnon, that's who." With a sigh, Aggie brushed her fingers against her beehive hairdo, tinted purple this week. "I've been attracted to that man ever since his wife died, and we're good friends. I call him a lot, and sometimes he calls me. He's such a good listener. When we're talking together, my loneliness just melts away like butter in the hot sun." She paused. "But he never pays me no mind in a romantic way. I'm just his good friend—like a sister." Another sigh escaped her tangerine-painted lips.

Tonya already knew Aggie was smitten with Bruce. Last summer Callie had enlightened her about Aggie's interest, and most of the town knew Aggie pestered the man.

The bell jingled above the door, and they both turned as

Murray Twichell walked in.

Tonya frowned. *What's he doing here?*

Aggie rose from her chair. "Hey there, Murray. Did Clint close the barbershop today?"

"Not that I know of." Murray hung his coat on a hook by the door. "I'm a repeat customer. I liked the way Tonya cut my hair last month, so I thought I'd come back."

"Good thing you didn't preface it with a speeding ticket." Aggie cackled at her own joke. "But you're right on, Murray. Tonya's the best in the business."

Tonya didn't know whether to thank Aggie for the compliment or yell at her for bringing up her shortcomings. She pulled the cape from her chair and waited as Murray took a seat. As she pumped up the chair with her foot, she noticed that he wasn't wearing any aftershave. Instead he smelled clean, like soap.

Her eyes met his in the mirror. "So you want the same cut I gave you last time?"

Murray smiled. "That would be great, Tonya. You're the best, just like Aggie said."

Why is he being so nice?

As Tonya spritzed his hair with water, Aggie sat down on the other chair. "How's your mother, sugar?" The older woman leaned toward him. "Is the Parkinson's getting any worse?"

Murray shrugged. "She's about the same. She has that jumpy type of Parkinson's, and sometimes she's more nervous than at other times."

Picking up her shears, Tonya only half-listened as Aggie and Murray conversed about Priscilla Twichell's medications, the nursing home in Douglas, and the snowy weather. Tonya's thoughts kept drifting to Poe. What was he doing right now? What did he look like? She pictured him as a tall, handsome man—like Cary Grant. In her mind Tonya reviewed Poe's e-mails, which she'd read so many times she had them memorized. What had he thought about her comments last night?

Aggie sat back in her chair. "Thanks for updating me on your mother, Murray. Hope I'm not being too nosy. Sometimes Bruce says I'm just a mite too curious."

Tonya's attention shot back to the conversation. "We have to get you and Bruce together, Aggie."

Frowning, Aggie folded her arms. "I told you about that in confidence, Tonya Brandt."

Murray grinned. "About you and Bruce? Come on, Aggie, the entire town knows you like him." He glanced at Tonya in the mirror. "You're right. It's time those two got together."

"Well I never!" Aggie sputtered. "We're just good friends, that's all."

"But Aggie. . ." Tonya clipped the hair around Murray's right ear. "Don't you want to be more than good friends?"

"Hey, I could talk to Bruce." Murray raised his eyebrows. "Maybe he just needs a push in the right direction."

"Murray's right, Aggie. Bruce is very laid-back. You two will be friends forever—and friends only—if someone doesn't nudge him toward you."

Aggie's chubby face flushed. "But, you see. . .it's just that. . ." Her bracelets clinked together as she raised her hands, then dropped them. "I don't want him to think I'm *pushy* or anything."

Murray grinned, and Tonya felt his shoulders shake in silent laughter. Biting her lower lip, Tonya tried to hide her own smile and concentrate on the haircut.

Aggie, oblivious to their amusement, paced behind Tonya. "What if Bruce don't want a closer friendship? And if I push him—why, he might never speak to me again!"

Tonya shook her head. "He probably knows how you feel already. If he's truly your friend, he's not going to suddenly hate you if you want to get closer."

"I agree with Tonya." Murray's eyes followed the pacing Aggie in the mirror. "If you want me to, I'll put a bug in his ear. I see him most mornings at the Trailblazer Café. On the other hand, if you're dead set against it. . ." He shrugged.

Twisting her hands, Aggie stopped and threw a desperate look at Tonya.

"Go for it, Aggie!" Tonya grinned. "This might be the chance of a lifetime."

"Oh okay." She pursed her orange lips. "Just promise me, Murray, that you'll talk to him in private. I don't want the whole place to know I'm pining after him."

"You have my word."

Tonya unfastened the cape and pulled it from Murray's neck. "All finished."

"I'll meet you up at the front, Murray." Aggie waddled to the cash register. "Do you want to buy any other products? Shampoo? Conditioner?" She seemed ready to dismiss Bruce as a topic of conversation.

He stood. "No thanks." Smiling at Tonya, he pulled his wallet from his back pocket. "Thanks for the great job, Tonya."

Grabbing a broom, she nodded. She had left the top a little longer, and it made him look good. Not handsome, of course—Murray would never be handsome.

After he left the shop, Tonya gazed at Murray's hair in the dustpan before she threw it in the trash. "You know, Aggie, I always thought Murray's hair was red, but it's really auburn. Almost brown."

"Growing darker with his age, I reckon. That kid used to be a carrottop, just like his mother. He's the spitting image of Priscilla." Aggie sighed as she took a seat in the other chair. "I feel so sorry for her with that Parkinson's. When I moved to Fort Lob, she was the first person who befriended me in this town. She prayed with me and helped me through some hard trials."

Tonya opened the closet door to put the broom away. "Did you have problems when you lived in Texas, Aggie?"

"Oh, hon, you don't want to know. Suffice it to say, I was running from a bad situation." She sighed. "But Priscilla— bless her heart. She soon had her own share of troubles, and I was comforting *her*."

"I remember when Murray's dad died."

"That ain't the half of it, sugar! So many people died in their family, one right after the other." Aggie counted off on her fingers. "Her father, his mother, her sister, her mother, his uncle—why, I believe we were going to a funeral for the Twichell family every month there for a while."

"How sad!" Tonya sank down on the other chair. "And then Murray's dad died, too."

"Yeah, a few years after all them other relatives died. Anson was quite a bit older than Priscilla, you know."

"I always liked Mrs. Twichell." Tonya reached back in her memory. "Sometimes Callie and I played at Murray's house, and Mrs. Twichell always had cookies for us. She was so nice to me, especially when Murray and Callie ignored me. I was a little pest to them since I was three years younger."

Aggie smiled. "And now you kids are all grown-up." She glanced out the big plate-glass windows. "It's snowing again. Why don't you hightail it home, Tonya? We probably won't have much business between now and five."

"Thanks, Aggie." Tonya stood. "I want to see if Poe wrote to me, and the sooner the better."

❧

Wow. Murray's jaw dropped as he read the e-mail. It worked! He had written a few sentences about his loneliness, and Tonya peeled back her heart for three pages.

He reread the lines that caught him off guard.

> *My sisters, Melissa and Callie, are both married, and Molly is getting married in a few weeks. I'm the only single sister now, with no prospect for a husband on the horizon. Sometimes I worry that I'll never get married. Sure, I can get a date in a heartbeat, but of all the guys I know, I can't find a kindred spirit—someone who wants to know the real me, someone who will love me for who I am.*

Murray sat back. Strange she should mention the very thing

he wanted to do—get to know the real Tonya underneath all that outward beauty.

But Tonya never getting married? That was crazy.

He highlighted that paragraph in his reply.

> *Tonya, you're so beautiful. Why do you think you'll never marry? There are probably a thousand guys out there who would love to marry you.*

His fingers paused above the keys. Did that include him? Would he love to marry Tonya Brandt, the spoiled baby of the Brandt family?

He deleted the word *thousand* and replaced it with *dozen.*

> *There are probably a dozen guys out there who would love to marry you.*

He nodded. Now if she had money and fame, a thousand guys might be standing on her doorstep.

With a grin, he finished the letter and shut down his computer. He had to get up early tomorrow. It was back to work for the weekend, and he had to be in Cheyenne at seven in the morning. At least he had Monday off.

His twenty-seventh birthday.

ten

Murray sat at the kitchen table on Monday morning and finished his breakfast—a bowl of toasted oats with a few raspberries thrown in. As he ate, he perused *The Scout*, Fort Lob's newspaper.

It didn't seem like his birthday, although on Friday he had received a card from his secret pal along with a devotional book. He wasn't sure who his secret pal was, but the writing was definitely feminine.

He wished his mom were here to pamper him and bake him a cake, but after lunch he planned to visit her at the Pine River Nursing Home in Douglas. Maybe the nurses would sing "Happy Birthday." At least they did last year.

The wall phone above the counter rang.

He lifted his eyes from the paper. Who could that be? The landline rang so seldom. After the second ring, he stood and grabbed the receiver. "Hello?"

"Hey, Twitch!" Derek Brandt's voice sounded in his ear. "We missed you at church yesterday."

"I had to work all weekend, which really bummed me out. I hate missing church."

"I figured that must be the culprit. Just wanted to tell you about the Single Servings Valentine's party. Originally we planned it for February fourteenth, but as you know, my sister's getting married on that day."

Murray took a seat at the table. "Yeah, I have to go to Douglas and get fitted for my tux."

"Me, too—unfortunately." Derek laughed. "Anyway, the class decided to move the party up to February seventh, and we're going to reveal the secret pals then. I hope you can come."

Murray nodded. "I'll see if I can get a couple hours off that day."

"Are you off today?"

"Yeah." Murray held in a sigh, thinking of the slow day ahead of him.

"Mom wanted me to invite you over for supper tonight— for your birthday." Derek chuckled. "Happy birthday, Twitch!"

"Oh thanks! I'm surprised someone remembered." His mood ratcheted up a notch.

"Mom's a walking calendar—she remembers every birthday and anniversary of everyone we know." Derek paused. "After supper Dad and I are planning to watch the play-off game from last night. Since we were in church, Dad recorded it. You're welcome to stay and watch it with us if you want."

"Sure, that would be great!" Murray glanced at the newspaper. "I already know who won, but I'll watch it anyway."

"Hey, don't give it away!" Derek laughed. "Dad and I refuse to look at a paper or turn on the radio until we see the game on the DVR tonight."

Murray chuckled. "Okay." This would be a good birthday after all.

⋅⋅

Tonya entered the den holding a plate of brownies. She stopped in the doorway to survey the three men watching the football game. Dad sat in the recliner, his feet up. Derek and Murray sat on either end of the couch, each holding a can of soda. All three had their eyes glued to the action on the big-screen TV. Memories of Reed Dickens—sitting in the exact spot Murray now occupied—filled her mind, and she was glad she wasn't trying to impress anyone tonight.

"Here are the brownies." She set the plate on the coffee table.

"Brownies?" Dad pulled a fake frown. "We just celebrated Murray's birthday with cake and ice cream. How do you expect us to eat brownies?"

Tonya shrugged. "It's a tradition. I always make brownies when you guys watch football."

"I'll eat one." Derek snatched it off the plate. "I love these."

Murray leaned forward and picked up a brownie. "Are these the same kind you made for the Christmas party?"

"Yep, my secret recipe with chocolate chunks and cream cheese."

"These are fantastic! I wanted to take the last one at the party, but Aggie beat me to it." Murray took a bite and chewed a moment. "You should call them Tonya's Terrific Brownies."

A warm feeling filled Tonya at his praise. "Well, you don't have to worry about Aggie eating them up tonight." She turned to the door. "Enjoy."

"Hey!" Dad called after her. "Aren't you going to watch the game with us?"

Tonya turned back. "I'm not really into football, Dad." *And I don't want to sit beside Murray.*

"Come on." Murray moved over and patted the sofa cushion between him and Derek.

"Yeah, sis." Derek motioned to her. "Come watch the game with us. The more the merrier."

Tonya raised her eyebrows, then shrugged. She had nothing else to do and was soon settled between her brother and Murray.

This promised to be a boring evening.

"Did you see that, Twitch?" Derek pointed to the screen. "We did that exact same play one time against Northern."

Murray laughed. "I was thinking the same thing. And remember that game we played against Pinedale? Fourteen to twenty with only a half minute left, and you threw me that Hail Mary right down the middle of the field."

"Oh, that was a great game." Derek's shoulder brushed Tonya's as he leaned forward. "You made the touchdown with fifteen seconds to spare, and then we got the extra point and beat 'em by one point."

Tonya looked back and forth between the two men. "How do you guys remember all that? You played those games eight or nine years ago."

"You were there, Tonya." Murray's close-set blue eyes met hers. "Don't you remember? That was one of our biggest wins."

She smirked. "I was a cheerleader, not a statistician."

"I still remember the scores of all our games, especially during my senior year." Murray raised his eyebrows. "Don't you remember stuff from high school?"

"Well, I remember what I wore to the prom my senior year." She thought back to the dark blue sequined dress she had made herself. "And I loved my shoes." Whatever happened to those strappy blue shoes?

Murray pointed to the screen. "Hey, watch that guy go. He's fast!"

Tonya studied Murray's hand until he dropped it back to his leg. She had never noticed his hands before—strong, masculine hands with just a hint of dark red hair across the back, thick fingers, and clean square nails.

The men discussed the game on TV before the talk turned once again to high school football.

"You were good, Murray." Dad reached over and grabbed a brownie. "In fact, you were probably the best wide receiver the school ever had."

"Well, I don't know. . . ."

"MVP your senior year." Derek glanced at him. "Don't be so humble, Twitch."

Humble? Tonya rolled her eyes. The words *humble* and *Murray* did not belong in the same sentence.

"What about you?" Murray motioned toward Derek. "You were voted MVP the next year. That school never had such a good quarterback."

Tonya looked straight ahead. "Let's just pat each other on the back."

"We are, Tonya." Murray leaned into her shoulder and lowered his voice. "And we can't forget the cheerleaders. Some of them were really pretty—especially that Brandt girl."

She tried not to smile, but didn't quite succeed. "Thanks."

He grinned at her, flashing those straight white teeth. Then, leaning forward, he looked at the screen.

She took a moment to study his profile. His eyelashes seemed darker than they used to be—the same dark auburn as his hair—and she had never noticed how long they were. His nose didn't look so big in profile, and his hair, which she had cut, was growing out nicely. A hint of beard showed beneath his cheeks, ending in a strong chin. Maybe he wasn't as homely as she had always thought.

He turned and looked at her. "Something wrong?"

Caught staring! Warmth crept up her neck, and she focused on the TV. "Nothing."

Murray picked up another brownie. "Why are you keeping this recipe a secret? These are the best brownies I've ever tasted."

She shrugged. He didn't need to know her dream about publishing her own cookbook someday.

As a football player ran in for a touchdown, both Murray and Derek shot to their feet.

"Great play!" Derek high-fived Murray. "Now the Cardinals are in the lead."

Murray resumed his seat. "According to the paper, that play was a turning point."

"Don't tell us!" Derek laughed.

As the men settled back on the sofa, Tonya stood. "I think I'll see what Mom is doing."

Derek swallowed a sip of soda. "Tell her to come in here and watch the game with us."

"Huh!" Dad reached for another brownie. "Fat chance of that. Your mother thinks football is a waste of time."

Like mother, like daughter. Leaving the room, Tonya's thoughts lingered on Murray. At least he hadn't ignored her all evening as Reed Dickens had. Murray liked her brownies and, she admitted, she enjoyed his company.

Passing the mirror hanging in the hallway, she stopped to study her reflection. Her dark hair still looked good, but her lipstick had faded and some of her eyelashes were sticking together. How did that happen?

But it didn't matter. Tonya planned to talk to Mom and then go to bed—after she checked her e-mail. Inexplicably, she hadn't heard from Poe all weekend. What if he had lost interest in her? That thought stopped her in her tracks, and she determined to write him every day until he replied.

As she made her way to the kitchen, she mused about Poe. Who was he? What did he look like? Murray's profile came to her mind. From the side, his face was almost handsome. If only his eyes weren't so close-set.

※

Murray booted up his computer. It was after midnight, but he didn't have to report to police headquarters in Cheyenne until three o'clock tomorrow afternoon. Tonya hadn't returned after she left the den, but maybe she wrote him an e-mail.

Folding his hands behind his head, he sat back in his chair. He hadn't enjoyed an evening like tonight in a long time. And on his birthday, too! He'd have to write a thank-you note to the Brandts, making sure to print of course.

His mail popped up with three new letters, all from Tonya Brandt. He forgot that he hadn't written her since Friday evening. And it never entered his mind to write this morning.

Clicking open the first letter, Murray skimmed through the first two pages—Tonya's usual surface talk. On page three, she finally commented on his letter from Friday night.

> *Thanks for the compliment that I'm beautiful, Poe. I've had a lot of dates in my life, but a dozen guys wanting to marry me? Oh sure—LOL.*
>
> *The men I've dated could be separated into two camps: the trophy-date types and the smoochers. Either a guy wants to show me off (a beautiful woman hanging on his arm), or he*

just wants to kiss me (and usually the feeling is not mutual).
No one cares about my mind or talents—what makes me tick
*on the inside. *sigh* It's hard to be beautiful.*

Murray frowned. He couldn't begin to fathom her predicament—good looks had never been his problem. But here was the real Tonya, revealing her heart, and he had no idea what to say.

His mind wandered back to the evening, sitting next to her on the sofa. He could understand why men would want to kiss her. When he had leaned toward her and gazed into her beautiful dark blue eyes, kissing her was the first thought that popped into his mind.

But he wasn't going to toy with her emotions. If he ever kissed Tonya, it would be because he loved her for who she was on the inside, and he would know that she loved him and wanted to kiss him back.

When I fall in love, it will be forever.

The words of the old song ran through his mind, and he hummed a few lines before he expelled a long sigh. It would never be with Tonya.

eleven

Sitting at the kitchen table on Tuesday morning, Tonya carefully applied a coat of fuchsia rose to her fingernails. "If only I could grow them longer, but it's hard to play the piano with long nails. They have a tendency to click on the keys."

Mom looked up from the letter she penned to Grandma. "You have such pretty hands, honey."

"Yeah, as long as I don't have any warts." Splaying her fingers, Tonya inspected them but didn't see any telltale bumps.

The back door opened, and Derek walked in. "Here's the mail."

Mom stopped writing. "It came this early?" She glanced at the clock above the stove. "It's only eight fifteen."

"No, this is yesterday's mail. I forgot to pick it up before supper last night since Twitch was here." He set several envelopes and a magazine beside Mom, then threw an envelope toward Tonya. It landed near her nail polish bottle. "A letter for you, sis."

Leaning over, she looked at the envelope as she waved her hands back and forth. "There's no return address, but it's not from Poe. The handwriting is too wavery." She glanced up at Derek. "Could you open it for me?"

"Women and their fingernails," he muttered. Tearing open the envelope, he pulled out a card and began reading silently.

"Derek! You were supposed to open it, not read it." Tonya grabbed the card, hoping her nails were dry.

Her brother grinned as he left the room. "It's from your secret pal."

As Tonya opened the card, a bookmark fell to the table. She picked it up. "I love bookmarks. It says, 'Tonya: praiseworthy.

81

A woman that feareth the Lord, she shall be praised. Proverbs 31:30.'" Silently she read the spidery penmanship. *I'm praying for you. Have a wonderful day. Your secret pal.* She passed the card to her mom. "Who do you think wrote this? It looks like my secret pal is eighty years old."

Mom studied it. "Hmmm. . .maybe Horace Frankenberg. He has shaky handwriting."

"Horace? I hope not."

Her mother smiled at her. "You'll have to wait until next week when you find out at the party." She folded the letter she'd been writing.

Tonya took the card and bookmark. "Well, it doesn't matter if that old bachelor is my secret pal. I have Poe now."

Mom frowned. "Have you sent anything to your secret pal? Isn't it Murray?"

She nodded. "Murray's my *receiver*—which is a stupid label, but Reed Dickens made it up. I've sent Murray several cards, plus I sent him that devotional book through the mail for his birthday. Remember? And I already bought his gift for the Valentine's party." Standing, she grabbed the nail polish bottle. "I'd better hurry. Don't want to be late for work."

⁊⧫

Two hours later Tonya closed the cash register at The Beauty Spot. "Thanks, Charlotte. See you in six weeks."

Charlotte Eschbach touched her newly permed coiffure. "Good job, as usual, Tonya."

As Charlotte left the building, Tonya took a seat on the stool behind the cash register, thankful for a moment's rest. It had been another busy morning. Aggie stood at her workstation, positioning curlers into Gloria Schutzenhofer's weekly set, and the two of them chatted away, oblivious to anything else.

The bell above the door jingled, and Murray strode in. He glanced once at Aggie, then motioned for Tonya to come to the door.

She walked to the waiting area.

Turning his back to the room, he dropped his voice. "I

talked to Bruce this morning about dating Aggie."

Tonya's eyebrows lifted. "And?"

"He's open to it." Murray leaned closer, and his breath fanned her face. It smelled sweet, like mint. "But he doesn't like her outdated hairstyle and loud makeup. He said if she would change a few things, he might ask her out."

Tonya glanced back at the two women. Still deep in conversation, they didn't notice the tête-à-tête going on by the door. "I'll talk to her."

"People don't change easily, but I suppose it's worth a try. I'll work on Bruce."

"Okay." She smiled. "This might be fun."

Murray grinned. "It'll be interesting, to say the least. See you later." He strode out the door.

A feeling of peace settled over Tonya as she watched him get in his patrol car and drive away. Murray was no longer the boy who tormented her; he was actually a very nice guy. And he must be a romantic at heart, wanting to get Bruce and Aggie together. That thought surprised her. He always tried to act so macho, but maybe she didn't know the real Murray.

As she walked back to the cash register, Poe entered her thoughts. Now there was a true romantic soul. Did he know Aggie and Bruce? She would tell Poe about them and ask his advice on the best way to convince Aggie to change.

❧

I thought it might be fun if we could instant message each other every evening. Say nine o'clock?

Excitement buzzed through Tonya as she read Poe's e-mail. Instant messaging with him would almost be like talking on the phone. But then she frowned. How did someone do instant messaging? She was on Facebook, and she exchanged text messages with a few friends from her cell phone, but she'd never tried to instant message.

Dashing downstairs, she found her mother in the laundry

room. "Mom, where's Derek?"

"In the barn with Dad." Mom scattered laundry soap in the washer. "What do you need?"

"Instant messaging."

Mom's eyebrows dipped in a frown. "Never heard of it."

Tonya grinned. "I figured you wouldn't know."

"What is it?"

"Tell you later." Tonya left the room. "I'll get Derek to help me."

Making her way through the kitchen, she paused to open the oven door. The smell of roasted chicken greeted her, and her stomach growled in return. Hopefully Derek could show her how to instant message before supper.

She entered the mudroom. Mom's old winter coat hung on a hook beside the door, and Tonya slipped it on before making her way outside.

Low clouds hung heavy with snow in the coming twilight. The wind whistled past her ears, and she hunched her shoulders as she walked the hard dirt path that led to the barn.

The large sliding doors were shut, so Tonya opened the side door to enter. The warmth of the barn enveloped her, along with the smells of leather and horses.

Derek exited one of the horse stalls. "Hey, sis. What are you doing here?"

"Do you know how to instant message?"

"On a computer?"

"Yeah." Tonya moved toward him. "Poe wants to instant message every evening at nine o'clock, but I don't know how to do it."

Derek shrugged. "You need an account. Ask Dad to help you."

"Ask me what?" Dad's heavy boots clomped around the corner on the concrete floor.

Tonya turned to him. "Do you have an instant message account, Dad?"

"A what?" Dad looked as perplexed as Mom had.

Tonya sighed. "This family is so computer illiterate."

"Call Twitch." Derek walked back to the stall. "He'll explain it to you."

"Yep." Dad nodded. "If it's about computers, Murray will know."

❧

Murray placed his supper dishes in the kitchen sink just as the phone rang. He raised his eyebrows. Two phone calls in two days. How amazing was that?

He picked up the receiver. "Hello?"

"Murray, this is Tonya."

Tonya is calling me? The force of the surprise pushed him back against the counter. "Oh, um, hi, Tonya. How are you?"

"Murray, I need to instant message someone, but no one in my family has a clue how it's done, and I really need to find out before this evening."

He grinned. "Instant messaging, huh? Do you have an account?"

"I don't think so." She sounded perplexed. "How long does it take to get one?"

"Oh, three minutes at the most. I could walk you through it. Do you want me to come over?"

"That would be great." Relief poured through her words. "The sooner, the better."

"I'll be there in ten minutes." He hung up the phone—and laughed.

❧

Tonya: *So how should I approach Aggie about changing her hairstyle? She's been wearing her hair in this whipped-up beehive for years. Being a beautician, she thinks she has a corner on style, and she can be very stubborn.*

Tonya hit the RETURN button, then sat back to wait for Poe's reply. Glancing at the clock beside her bed, she was surprised that it was almost eleven. They'd been instant messaging, which Poe called "IMing," for almost two hours.

And she had to get up early for work tomorrow. She threw on her *I Love Lucy* pajamas. By that time Poe had replied.

Poe: *It sounds like Bruce doesn't want to have a 1960s fashion queen hanging on his arm. LOL He wants his date to live in the twenty-first century, and in that case, Aggie could either win or lose Bruce on her hairstyle alone. If you convinced her of that, she would probably be willing to try something new.*

Positioning her fingers on the keyboard, Tonya started typing.

Tonya: *You are one smart guy! I'll try to convince her. Thanks for the advice!*
Poe: *You're welcome.*
Tonya: *I hate to end our first conversation, but I need to get to bed. Tomorrow is a workday for me.*
Poe: *I have off tomorrow. You certainly don't need your "beauty sleep" since you are extremely beautiful, but I'll let you go. Good night.*
Tonya: *Wait! What do you do for a living?*
Poe: *Haha! Wouldn't you like to know?*
Tonya: *Yes, I would!*
Poe: *Sorry, classified information. Let's IM tomorrow night at nine. Good night.*
Tonya: *Good night, Poe.*

With a sigh, she shut down her computer. Who in the world was this guy? And how many days or weeks would pass before she found out?

ঽ

"Change my hairstyle?" Aggie's ultra-blue eyelids widened as she stared at Tonya. "Do you know how ugly I am with flat hair? Why, the birds would stop singing, the stars would stop shining if I were to let my hair down. No, no, no." She ambled to the broom closet. "If Bruce don't like me the way I am, he can go fish for someone else."

Tonya rolled her eyes. *Stubborn woman!* "Listen, let me fix your hair and do your makeup for one date—just for one evening. Then the next morning, you can style your hair any way you want."

The broom swished as Aggie swept up after their last customer. Tonya stepped back so she wouldn't inhale the tiny curls that were flying through the air. When Aggie said nothing, Tonya made another attempt to appeal to her reason.

"Don't you think Bruce is worth it, Aggie? I mean, look at him—such a handsome, dignified man. I'm sure you'd love to be hanging on his arm at some sophisticated restaurant. And you'll want to look like you belong in the twenty-first century, cultured and refined—"

"Instead of looking like the hick that I am." Aggie's eyes spit fire as she stared at Tonya.

"That's not what I meant." Tonya sank down on a chair. "But Bruce has very particular tastes. You, of all people, should know that."

The broom handle hit the floor as Aggie dropped into the other chair. "Oh, I suppose you're right." Her shoulders drooped. "Maybe it ain't gonna work out between us after all. We just come from two different worlds."

"It can work, Aggie." Tonya leaned forward. "Bruce only wants you to tone down your makeup a bit, and. . .and step out of the '60s with your hairstyle. He's a very reserved gentleman, and he doesn't want to be noticed." She thought on that a moment. "Although he's so dignified and good-looking, people notice him anyway."

"Don't I know it!" Aggie paused. "I suppose I could change for him." The stubborn glint returned to her eyes. "But only for one date, mind you."

"That's all he's asking." Tonya gave an inward sigh of relief.

Now to talk to Murray.

twelve

At the Valentine's party on Saturday, Murray unwrapped his gift as the Single Servings watched. They were taking turns opening their gifts, and after the gift was opened, the secret pal would reveal his or her identity.

Derek had told Murray that he wanted a comfortable place to have the Valentine's party, but he didn't want to move all the furniture to the church again. So here they were, crowded into the Brandts' living room. Murray sat on the same blue chair as before. Most of the men sat on straight chairs they had dragged in from the dining room. Across from Murray, Tonya sat on the sofa between Cheyenne and Laurie Smullens. Laurie and Reed had recently broken up as a couple, and Reed seemed to be scouting out other possibilities. Near the fireplace, he sat beside Gretchen Hughes, the quietest woman ever born, and tried to engage her in conversation.

Murray finally pulled the gift wrap off his present, revealing an atomic watch. "Wow, this is nice!" Raising his eyebrows, he glanced around the room.

Tonya smiled. "It's from me, Murray. I was your secret pal."

His lips parted. Tonya was his secret pal, and he was hers? "Thanks for the watch, Tonya. This is great. I really like it."

Nodding, she looked down and her face tinged pink.

Murray gazed at her. *Tonya—embarrassed?* Or was it humility? She didn't realize how much humility complemented her beauty.

Derek sat on a straight chair near the fireplace. "Okay, Tonya. Why don't you open your gift now?"

As Tonya savagely tore the paper from the gift Murray had painstakingly wrapped, he glanced at Derek. Had Tonya's brother purposely set them up as each other's secret pal? Murray would ask Derek later how that came about. He couldn't picture Derek trying to play matchmaker.

"Oh!" Tonya's pretty eyes widened. "It's a book of hymn arrangements for the piano. Oh, I love it!" She glanced around, her eyes landing on the men near the dining room. "Horace, did you give this to me?"

Horace? Murray looked across the room at the man in question.

Horace looked just as surprised. "No, my secret pal is, um, well, he didn't open his gift yet, so I can't say."

Tonya's face reddened once more. "Sorry, I was just guessing, but evidently I guessed wrong." She looked around the room. "Anyone?"

Trying to hide his grin, Murray wished he could make her squirm a few more minutes, but he spoke up. "It's from me, Tonya."

"You?" Tonya's mouth dropped open. Then she clamped it shut and looked at her brother. "Derek! How come I was Murray's secret pal and he was mine? Did you do that on purpose?"

Derek raised his hands as if trying to fend her off. "Hey, don't blame me! The identity of everyone's secret pal is a surprise to me, too. Mom put all the secret pals together, and she was the only one who knew who they were."

"Mom, huh? Okay."

Tonya looked back at Murray, and he could almost read her mind. He wouldn't put it past Mrs. Brandt to play the matchmaker role either.

Tonya sighed. "Well, thanks for the piano book, Murray." She smiled, and her entire demeanor changed. "This looks like a great book. I can't wait to play these songs."

He nodded. "You're welcome."

As someone else took a turn unwrapping a gift, Murray kept his eyes on Tonya. She opened the piano book and studied the table of contents, then spoke to Cheyenne in low tones.

Murray thought about the letters they had e-mailed each other, about their own matchmaking efforts for Aggie and Bruce, about working with her on her computer, and the instant messaging they had done that week.

A strange realization hit him. *I really care for her.* He wasn't sure if it was love, but his feelings for her were definitely changing.

❧

On Monday morning, Tonya wielded her shears on seven-year-old Kylie Ewing's long blond hair. She smiled, thinking how cute Kylie would look once her hair was cut to frame her heart-shaped face.

Aggie stood at the other chair, working on Kylie's mom's hair. The bell above the door jingled, and both Tonya and Aggie looked up as Murray entered. He was dressed in his uniform, so Tonya knew he hadn't come in for a haircut.

"Hey, Murray," Aggie called. "What can we do for you?"

He hesitated. "I see you're both busy. I'll come back."

"Just a minute." Leaving her station, Tonya joined Murray, dropping her voice to a whisper. "Is this about Aggie and Bruce?"

He grinned, lowering his voice as well. "He agreed to take her out."

"Really?" She bit back a smile.

"I'll call you later about the details." Murray backed toward the door, now speaking in a normal voice. "Say, a half hour?"

Tonya nodded. "That would be fine."

He left, and she went back to Kylie's hair. Aggie kept glancing at her but didn't ask any questions. Tonya just smiled.

❧

By the time the Ewing ladies left, Aggie had another customer. As Tonya swept the floor, the phone rang.

"I'll get it, Aggie." Walking behind the cash register, she picked up the receiver. "The Beauty Spot, this is Tonya."

"Hey, Tonya, it's Murray."

With a wistful sigh, she sank on the stool behind the counter. His voice was amazing. Every time they spoke on the phone, she thought again of how much she loved that baritone. Too bad he didn't have an ultra-handsome face to go with it. "What's the news?"

"If Aggie tones down the makeup and changes her hairstyle, Bruce agreed to take her to Phoebe's."

"Phoebe's? In Lusk?" Tonya's shoulders slumped. "But that's a diner—with a counter and stools. I wanted him to take her to some sophisticated restaurant in Cheyenne with linen tablecloths and good silverware."

"It's a start, okay? You wouldn't believe how much I had to talk him into this. And we settled on Tuesday night, mainly so he couldn't change his mind."

"Tuesday? You mean tomorrow night?"

"Exactly. Do you think she can be ready by then?"

Tonya glanced at Aggie's green teased-up hair, her green eyelids decorated with silver sparkles, her wrinkled rouged cheeks and orange lips. Dropping her voice, Tonya spoke into the phone. "She'll be ready. I'll make sure of that."

"Good. Uh, Tonya—Bruce has a stipulation for this date. He wants you and me to go along."

Tonya frowned. "Why? Do they need chaperones?"

Murray chuckled. "Not as chaperones, Tonya—as a double date. You know—Aggie and Bruce, you and me." He paused. "Would you be willing to be my date tomorrow night?"

Tonya's lips parted. A date with Murray Twichell?

"It was Bruce's idea," he continued. "I think he's nervous about dating Aggie—or *Agatha,* as he calls her. He probably wants us to be there in case he runs out of things to say."

Listening to Murray's smooth baritone voice in her ear, Tonya's defenses weakened. Why shouldn't she go on a date with him? They were good friends now. "Sure, Murray, I'll be your date."

"Thanks." He sounded relieved. "Bruce and I already talked about the car situation. At first he wanted to drive his

Buick so he'd have something to do while we traveled, but I talked him out of it. Now I'm going to drive my SUV, and Bruce will sit in the back with Aggie."

"That's good." Tonya couldn't imagine sitting with Murray in the backseat for a half hour with nothing to do.

"Here's another stipulation Bruce wants—I'm to pick you up first, then we'll drive to his house to pick him up, and then go to Aggie's house. So we'll pick her up last and drop her off first."

Tonya puffed out a laugh. "Boy, he must be nervous." But if Bruce had stipulations, why couldn't she? "Um, Murray, if you want me to go with you, I don't want to go to Phoebe's. Let's go to The Four Seasons in Cheyenne."

"Are you crazy? That's the most expensive restaurant in the city."

"Which is exactly why we should go there." She took a deep breath. "Bruce needs to show Aggie that she's worth spending money on." *And so am I.*

"I don't know if Bruce will agree to that."

Tonya raised her eyebrows. "We'll surprise him. After all, Murray, you're the driver."

"A surprise, huh?" She heard the smile in his voice. "All right, Tonya. We'll do it. Could I pick you up at five?"

"How about five thirty? I have to work until five, although I have a feeling I'll spend most of the day working on Aggie's hair and makeup."

"Five thirty, then, at your house. Be sure to tell Aggie."

"I'll give her the message. Uh, Murray, now I have a question for you."

"What's up?"

"It's about the secret pal thing. You sent me a card last week with very wavery handwriting." She gave a little laugh. "I thought it was from Horace Frankenberg, but it must have been from you."

"So that's why you thought Horace was your secret pal."

"Did you write that card, Murray?"

"No, I was visiting my mom in the nursing home, and I asked her to sign it."

"Oh." No wonder it looked like it was written by an eighty-year-old person. Mrs. Twichell must not be eighty yet, but she had Parkinson's, which made her hands shake.

A strong desire came over Tonya to see Mrs. Twichell again. Perhaps she could talk Derek into letting the Single Servings visit the nursing home in Douglas one of these days. "That was nice of your mom to write the card. Thank her for me."

"I'll do that." He paused. "Well, I'll pick you up at five thirty tomorrow, and you don't have to change a thing for me. I mean—don't whip your hair up into a honeycomb."

She laughed. "It's a *beehive*, but don't worry. I would never tease up my hair like that."

He chuckled. "Until tomorrow then."

Bidding him good-bye, Tonya hung up and glanced at Aggie. She already knew how she would change Aggie's hairstyle and makeup. This date with Bruce was so important. It might even be a turning point for them.

Tonya was glad she would be along. Now she could witness Bruce's reaction to the new and improved Aggie firsthand. And she and Murray hadn't argued for weeks.

It would be an interesting evening.

thirteen

That evening Tonya stood to stretch in front of her computer as she waited for Poe's next comment to pop up. They had been IMing for an hour already.

> Poe: *Let's share a secret or two that we want to keep private. OK?*

Tonya took her seat. A secret? Well, why not? She began to type.

> Tonya: *OK, you go first.*
> Poe: *My mom taught me to crochet when I was a kid, and to be honest, I really like it. Sometimes I'll grab a ball of yarn and a crochet hook while I'm watching an old movie, just to have something to do with my hands.*
> Tonya: *You're kidding!*
> Poe: *Don't tell anyone! It will ruin my macho image.*

With a laugh, she shook her head.

> Tonya: *How can I tell anyone? No one knows who you are.*
> Poe: *I do have that advantage. What's your secret?*
> Tonya: *Warts! When I was a little girl, someone threw a toad down my shirt, and that toad gave me warts on my fingers.*
> Poe: *Warts, huh? Was this "someone" a little boy who wanted the attention of a pretty little girl?*

Tonya frowned. That's exactly what Aggie had said in Murray's defense.

> Tonya: *How did you know?*
> Poe: *It's a common pastime of young boys—tormenting little girls they like. Ten years later, they change their tactics and give flowers.*
> Tonya: *LOL. Now I want you to share another secret. What do you look like? Describe your face to me.*

Smiling, she sat back. It would be interesting to see him get out of this one.

Poe: *I am seven shades of ugly.*

Tonya: *No you're not. Who do you look like?*

Poe: *Reed Dickens.*

Tonya's eyes widened. Was Poe actually Reed Dickens in disguise? That would be horrible! *I don't even like Reed!*

Tonya: *Tell me the truth—R U Reed?*

Poe: *You asked me who I looked like.*

Tonya: *Do you really look like him?*

Poe: *Hey, I'm seven shades of ugly, remember? But Reed can't help it if he's handsome. He's a great guy, too. Don't you think?*

Tonya: *No! I invited him to our house once, and he totally ignored me.*

Poe: *How could he ignore a beautiful woman like you?*

Tonya: *All he talked about was his ex-girlfriend. Then he claimed to be the great-grandson of Charles Dickens, and I believed him!*

Poe: *Haha! You should have beat the dickens out of him.*

Tonya: *Very funny.*

Poe: *Did I tell you I'm the great-grandson of Edgar Allan Poe?*

Tonya: *Very big LOL! I don't believe you for a second.*

Poe: *Smart gal.*

Five minutes later Poe signed off. Tonya was sorry to see him go, but she had to get to bed. Tomorrow was a big day. Aggie needed to look perfect for Bruce, and Tonya couldn't wait to visit The Four Seasons restaurant. A buzz of excitement ran through her. Tomorrow night would not only be interesting, but fun.

❧

Murray picked up the crochet hook from the end table. Why had he told Tonya he liked to crochet? No one knew about that hidden talent. But it didn't matter. She'd never find out he was her secret admirer.

He turned off the lamp beside the sofa. He couldn't believe Tonya still held that toad incident against him. They were just kids!

With a shake of his head, he trudged up the stairs to his bedroom. Work started at seven in the morning with road patrol. And then he had a hot date tomorrow night.

≈

The next morning Tonya pushed the accelerator as she raced along Antelope Road. Why didn't she get up the minute her alarm clock rang? Instead she hit the SNOOZE button—only it wasn't the SNOOZE button. She shut the thing off. If Mom hadn't woken her, she'd probably still be sleeping.

She glanced at the clock on the dashboard. Already ten minutes after nine and she needed to fix Aggie's hair and makeup today besides taking care of any customers who might wander into The Beauty Spot.

Good thing it wasn't snowing.

Pressing her lips together, Tonya tightened her grip on the steering wheel and pushed her right foot closer to the floorboard. As she sped past Road 334, the dirt road that led to the Carltons' ranch, she noticed a car in her peripheral vision.

A Wyoming highway patrol car.

A sinking feeling hit her stomach, and she glanced in the rearview mirror. Sure enough, red and blue lights began flashing as the car pulled onto Antelope Road.

Not again!

Slowing down, she pulled off to the side. The patrol car stopped behind her, the lights still flashing. Through the rearview mirror, she watched the patrolman exit his car, and her jaw dropped. She would recognize that auburn hair anywhere—hair she had cut!

Clamping her lips together, she hit the window button. She would give Murray a piece of her mind. How dare he give her a ticket when they were going out tonight!

But as he approached, she reconsidered. Truthfully, she had

been going way too fast, and Murray was just doing his job, as he told her before. With a humble attitude, perhaps she could talk him out of a ticket.

Tonya leaned out the window. "Murray, I'm sorry! Please don't ticket me. I accidentally overslept this morning, and I need to get to The Beauty Spot to work on Aggie's hair for tonight. So please, *please* let me go. Have mercy on me!"

Murray leaned one arm on the top of her car and gazed down at her. "I seem to recall this exact scene happening last December over on Main Street, but I don't think you learned your lesson, Tonya. Just now you were going eighty-one in a sixty-five zone." He raised his eyebrows. "In other words, you were breaking the law."

Folding her arms, all repentance fled. "I'm sorry, okay?"

"You don't sound sorry."

"Come on, Murray! Can't you let me off today? Please? I've already donated to the state of Wyoming."

"That was last year. As I said before, you've deserved a ticket many times when I've let you go." He held out his palm. "Now hand over your driver's license and registration."

≈

"And then, after he gave me that stupid ticket, he had the audacity to say, 'I'll pick you up at five thirty. I'm looking forward to our date tonight.'" Tonya squirted dark blond hair dye on Aggie's wet hair. "Can you believe that? As if I'm looking forward to dating *him* after he tickets me. And now I have to pay another eighty-five dollars to the state of Wyoming."

Sitting in the beautician chair, Aggie looked at Tonya in the mirror. "You just forget about that ticket, sugar. We'll all have a good time tonight."

"Easy for you to say." Tonya huffed out a breath. "You'd better keep an eye on me, Aggie. I might pull a butter knife on Murray and end up behind bars."

Aggie cackled out a laugh. "Oh, sugar, you'll have fun. Just like me. I'm praying for a wonderful time—in fact, a life-changing time with my Bruce."

"*Your* Bruce, is it?" In spite of her bad mood, Tonya smiled. "Don't you think you're jumping the gun a bit?"

"Not at all." Aggie's pale lips, devoid of lipstick, pulled into a frown. "I've been praying about Bruce and me for years. Waiting on the Lord—and on Bruce, too. And see how God has answered?" She laughed again. "We'll have so much fun, Bruce will be shocked. He'll see what he's been missing all these years. And it will be the same for you and your Murray."

"He's not my Murray." Tonya set the bottle of hair solution down, thankful she didn't have to breathe those ammonia fumes anymore.

Aggie gave her a knowing look. "Maybe someday."

"No way. This will be my one and only date with Murray Twichell. After tonight you and Bruce are on your own." She lifted the timer and set it. "Forty minutes, Aggie. While we're waiting, I'll do your nails."

Picking up a nail file, Tonya pushed Murray from her mind. At least she didn't have to deal with him until five thirty.

fourteen

Sitting behind the steering wheel of his SUV, Murray glanced sideways at his date. Tonya had not smiled once since he arrived at her house. Now they were driving to Bruce's ranch, which was four miles southwest of town, and she sat on the passenger side with her arms folded, holding a grudge.

The silence was awkward.

"Uh, Tonya, I know I'll see Aggie in a little while, but how did you fix her hair and makeup? Do you think Bruce will like it?"

Tonya's own makeup was flawless, as usual, and her dark hair looked perfect. She wore a blue dress that shimmered when she moved, along with the sapphire necklace he had given her. Murray certainly enjoyed the view of his date, although the conversation was less than stellar.

"Bruce will love her style." Tonya kept her eyes on the windshield, but the hint of a smile graced her rosebud lips. "You won't believe she's the same person when you see her. I permed her hair and teased it a few inches—instead of a foot, like she does." She turned toward him. "But it's the makeup that really improves her looks. I chose a foundation that matched her skin tone exactly, with deeper rouge for her cheeks and a dark plum lipstick. Then I worked on her eyes—much more subtle than the way she paints them. No sparkles or loud colors. Instead I chose a tan for her lids with a light mauve under her brows to highlight and a dark brown mascara."

Murray had no idea what she was talking about, and furthermore, he didn't care. He was just thankful she was talking. "That's great, Tonya. You must be good at that sort of thing."

" 'That sort of thing' is very important, Murray. A woman's makeup can make a real difference in her looks."

He grinned. "I bet you're just as beautiful without any makeup at all."

"Ha!" A pleased expression crossed her face before she turned to the window. "You'll never see me without makeup. I refuse to leave home without it."

Their conversation continued as Murray drove to Bruce's ranch and pulled into his driveway. He stopped beside the two-story farmhouse.

Tonya glanced at her watch. "We're early. I'd rather wait in Bruce's living room than out here in the car." She touched the door handle.

Murray leaned toward her. "Hang on, Tonya. I'll get your door."

⁂

Tonya raised her eyebrows as she watched him walk around the front of the car. Murray was taking this date seriously. She sighed, asking God to forgive her for being selfish. *I'm not going to think about that stupid ticket.* She would have a good time tonight—for Aggie's sake.

She smiled as he held open her door. "Thank you, Murray."

Together they ascended the steps to the farmhouse and crossed the wide wooden porch. Murray lifted the brass knocker and rapped twice.

Bruce opened the door. "Good evening. Come on in." He grabbed a bouquet of yellow roses from the end table near the door. The roses were wrapped in clear cellophane.

Tonya smiled at him. "What pretty flowers, and yellow is Aggie's favorite color."

Bruce's handsome face looked a little pale. "To be honest, I'm a bit rusty on dating protocol." His Scottish burr sounded thicker than usual. "My hope is that Agatha will enjoy the flowers, and the evening."

"She will." Tonya's sister, Callie, always said Bruce MacKinnon reminded her of Clark Gable. Tonya saw a resemblance, although Bruce didn't have a mustache. But he stood straight and tall with a commanding presence. No wonder Aggie was attracted to him. If he were forty years younger, Tonya might be attracted to the man herself.

They talked together for a few minutes before Bruce looked at his watch. "Are we ready to go?"

Murray cracked his knuckles. "We'll all set, Bruce. Let's pick up Aggie."

A cloud of annoyance settled over Tonya, threatening to rain on her good mood. She hated Murray cracking his knuckles, and it brought all his faults to her mind. He was so stubborn about upholding the law, and then there was that strong aftershave he always wore.

They walked to the SUV. Opening the door behind the driver's seat, Bruce disappeared into the back. Murray and Tonya stopped beside the front passenger door, and she felt Murray place his hand on the small of her back as he leaned over to open it.

His face was close to hers, and she took a deep breath. *Hmmm. . .no strong fragrance.*

"Murray, you're not wearing aftershave." The words tumbled out of her mouth before she even thought. *What a stupid thing to say!*

His eyes met hers. "It made you sneeze, so I stopped wearing it—about a month ago."

"Oh." She thought back, realizing it was true. "That was thoughtful of you. Thanks."

He gave a little nod as his eyes held hers. "You're welcome." Then he opened the car door and waited while she got in.

Bruce cleared his throat. "I wish Murray had let me drive my car."

Tonya swiveled to face him. "Don't be nervous, Bruce. Aggie will talk enough for both of you."

"True." He looked out the window as Murray settled behind the steering wheel.

Within ten minutes, they were at Aggie's doorstep. Tonya

watched Bruce knock on her door and then enter the house. She turned to Murray. "I wonder why Bruce is so nervous. He and Aggie talk on the phone all the time. They're good friends."

Murray shrugged. "Maybe Bruce doesn't like change, and he's afraid their platonic relationship will turn into something more." He glanced toward the house. "I think he feels—whoa!" His jaw dropped. "Is that Aggie?"

Tonya looked toward the house in time to see Bruce and Aggie descend the porch steps. Aggie was wearing a green dress with a long jacket that had a slimming effect. Her light hair was still styled the way Tonya had fixed it, although Aggie had added a tiara that sparkled when she moved.

Tonya grinned. "Yep, that's her. She *would* have to add her own signature in her hairstyle with that tiara."

"Wow, you were right. She looks like a different person. Good job, Tonya!"

A warm feeling flowed through her at his praise. "Thanks."

Bruce opened the back door and Aggie slipped inside. "Good evening, ya'll!" There was a definite lilt in her voice.

Murray nodded at her. "Aggie, you look fantastic. You should wear your hair like that all the time."

With a smile she looked down, a faint blush spreading across her cheeks. "Aw, thanks, Murray. But I can't take any credit. Tonya's the expert on beauty and style."

"I know." Murray looked at Tonya and winked. "She looks great, too."

An unexpected flutter hit Tonya's stomach. But she didn't have time to dwell on the implications. Bruce got in, and Aggie started up the conversation as Murray started up the car. Tonya and Aggie did most of the talking while Murray and Bruce did most of the listening. Twice Tonya caught Bruce appraising Aggie with a slight smile on his face. Tonya drew in a satisfied breath.

When Murray turned onto the interstate, Bruce sat forward. "Murray, where are we going?"

"It's a surprise." Murray grinned at Tonya before glancing into the backseat. "I realize we agreed on a restaurant, Bruce, but Tonya and I decided on a better one in Cheyenne."

Bruce cocked an eyebrow at Tonya. "Well, all right."

She smiled. "You'll like it, Bruce." *I hope you don't mind paying twice as much!*

&

Murray exited the freeway and found The Four Seasons. As they entered the restaurant, the women decided to make a pit stop in the powder room, leaving Murray alone with Bruce in the lobby. With shiny marble floors and a chandelier hanging from the ceiling, it looked like they had stepped into a beautiful mansion. A sweeping staircase ascended to the second floor with a balcony overlooking the lobby.

"Sorry about the switch in restaurants, Bruce." Murray stuck his hands in his pockets, trying for a nonchalant look. "Since it was Tonya's and my idea, I'll pick up the tab."

"No, no." Bruce glanced around the lobby. "I'm glad we came here. I'll be more than happy to pay for Agatha and myself."

The ladies emerged from the restroom, and the waiter showed them to a table for four with a snowy linen tablecloth and good silverware.

Murray pulled out Tonya's chair and seated her while Bruce did the same for Aggie. *This is certainly better than Phoebe's.*

Sitting across the table from Tonya was the highlight of his evening—excellent food with beautiful company. The four of them talked about their mutual friends and families. Bruce told stories about his boyhood in Scotland, and Aggie regaled them with stories from Texas. Tonya even laughingly told them how Murray had chased her with a toad when they were children, although she didn't mention anything about warts.

Murray hadn't enjoyed himself so much for months. Not even his birthday at the Brandts' home could compare with dating Tonya. Could they possibly have a romantic relationship?

Leaving the restaurant a little after nine, they dropped Aggie off at her house. Murray drove Bruce home, and the man couldn't stop talking about the wonderful evening.

"I'm glad you insisted on that restaurant, Murray." Bruce sat back, relaxed. "The Four Seasons was an excellent choice."

"Actually, it was Tonya's idea." Murray winked at her. "And don't you think those two women are worth it?"

"Oh, most definitely. We had such an enjoyable evening."

Tonya just smiled.

A few minutes later Murray pulled the SUV into Bruce's driveway, and they bade him good-bye. On the way home, Tonya discussed the date, particularly how much Bruce enjoyed Aggie's new look.

"I think they're perfect together, don't you?"

He grinned. "Yeah, perfect." *Just like us.* He reveled in this side of Tonya, enjoying her enthusiasm in someone else's success.

They traveled in a comfortable silence for a mile before Tonya spoke up.

"Murray, I have a question to ask you."

He glanced at her. "What?"

"Could you please cancel my speeding ticket from this morning?" She leaned toward him and fluttered her eyelashes. "I learned my lesson. Honest. From now on, even if I'm late to work, I'll drive the speed limit."

With a sigh, he concentrated on his driving. She was so tempting. He wished he could pull her into his arms and kiss her and that she would passionately kiss him back. But he was just fooling himself. Tonya would never kiss him back.

He shrugged. "It's too late. The ticket's out of my hands now. But there is one thing you could try."

"What's that?" She leaned a little closer.

He glanced at her beautiful face, so close to his. "You could go to court and plead not guilty."

"Really?" A look of hope filled her eyes.

"But then, since you're guilty, I'd have to go and testify against you, and they would take my word over yours."

"Murray!" Folding her arms, she slumped back in her seat. "I thought we were friends. Why do you have to be so hard-hearted?"

"I'm upholding the law, Tonya. Just because you're my friend doesn't mean I'll let you off the hook when you break the law."

"I bet you would ticket your own mother."

Murray chuckled. "Yep—haul her to jail if I had to, but I can't imagine my mom breaking the speed limit. Her personality is different than yours, and I've discovered that people drive according to their personality."

"I suppose that's true." She sat up a little straighter. "Did you know that people play the piano according to their personalities?"

He grinned. "I've noticed that about you, too."

She raised her perfectly shaped eyebrows. "What is that supposed to mean?"

"You drive a car the same way you play the piano." Murray turned right on Antelope Road. "Just from listening to your piano playing, I can tell what kind of personality you have."

"So what kind is it?"

Self-confident. Aggressive. Proud. But he couldn't say that. "Uh, let's look at it this way. Right now I'm driving sixty-five miles per hour, which is the speed limit on this road." He glanced at her. "Do you think we're going too slow?"

She shrugged. "Not really."

"No, this is the correct speed you should drive on Antelope Road, just as you should play the piano at the correct speed on a hymn, such as 'Victory in Jesus.'"

Her eyes widened. "You were *dragging* that hymn, Murray. It sounded like the congregation was at a funeral."

"A funeral?" He felt his ire rise. "You were *racing* the tempo. The people couldn't even spit the words out."

"That's not true!" Tonya's voice rose a notch. "No one sang fast enough to have a problem with the words. The tempo on that hymn should be allegro, but half the congregation didn't know whether to follow you or me."

"Wasn't I the song leader?" Anger simmered as he thumped his chest. "You were supposed to follow me, not vice versa. If you had followed my leading, everything would have been fine."

"You were singing way too slow."

"That doesn't matter!" He glared at her before looking back at the road. "I was the song director—the person the congregation was supposed to follow. Why can't you understand that?"

"Wayne Holland never leads the hymns that slow." Folding her arms tightly, she turned toward the passenger window.

Murray glanced at her stiff back. Like air releasing from a balloon, his temper went flat. This argument was causing their relationship to race toward nonexistent. "All right, never mind."

A thick silence pervaded the car as he drove down the Brandts' driveway. As soon as he stopped, Tonya opened the passenger door.

"Thanks for the dinner." She didn't smile, and she didn't look at him. Instead she slammed the door and walked to the house.

Murray watched her disappear inside before releasing a long breath, which turned into a prayer. *Lord, why can't we get along?*

&.

Tonya closed the front door gently, hoping no one would hear her. She was in no mood to discuss her date with Murray. From the noise emanating from the den, Mom and Dad must be watching TV. Fortunately it would cover up any sounds she might make.

As she trudged up the stairs, her heart seemed to get heavier with each step. What a horrible end to the evening!

She entered her bedroom and glanced at her computer. *Poe.* That's who she wanted to pour out her heart to. But she'd have to wait until eleven o'clock, their agreed-on time, since she had told him she would be out tonight. If only she could call him, or better yet, talk face-to-face.

With a sigh, she dropped into the desk chair. Her Bible sat next to the computer, and her conscience hit her. She hadn't read God's Word for two days.

No wonder I'm a mess.

Glancing at the clock, she calculated forty-five minutes before Poe would get on his computer. She would read until then. Last week she had discovered that Poe was a Christian, which made her feel a hundred percent better about their relationship. And from some of the things they had discussed, she could tell he had an intimate relationship with the Lord. Poe would give her good advice about Murray.

Opening the Bible at the marker in First Samuel chapter sixteen, she read the story of Samuel seeking a new king among Jesse's sons. The words soon spoke to her.

Samuel looked at Eliab, the tall and handsome eldest son, and figured this was God's anointed. But the Lord told Samuel not to look on the man's countenance or his height because He had refused him. The Lord didn't see Eliab the way Samuel saw him. *"For man looketh on the outward appearance, but the Lord looketh on the heart."*

Tonya sat back. *The outward appearance.* To her that was the most important thing. Didn't she want a tall, handsome man to marry? But she had dated all the handsome men she knew, and they only cared about her beautiful face and good figure, not her heart. The only man who cared about her heart was Poe.

And Murray.

Tonya frowned. Murray? But she had to acknowledge it was true.

She thought back over the past few hours. Bruce was right—it was an enjoyable evening. The food was delicious, the atmosphere was perfect, and Tonya had enjoyed sitting across the table from Murray. He was a good conversationalist and seemed genuinely interested in her as a person. He never stared at her or made snide comments, as some of her past dates had done. Instead he was a gentleman in the best sense of the word.

She bowed her head. *Lord, please forgive me for only looking at the outward appearance.* How could she condemn those who were less than beautiful, as if it were their fault? God had created Murray's close-set eyes and long nose, but she hadn't thought about his looks one time while they were eating.

And what about Poe? Despite everyone's predictions about a predator who wanted to meet her in a dark alley, Poe didn't want to meet her at all. Since they had begun instant messaging, she had invited him over for dinner three times, but he turned her down every time.

There had to be a reason.

With a sigh, she removed the sapphire necklace and gazed at it. She was falling in love with Poetry Lover Guy—a man who knew her heart better than anyone else. A man who loved the Lord and who cared about her. And she cared about him, no matter who he was.

If only she knew.

fifteen

At the wedding rehearsal on Friday night, the pastor at the Douglas church looked up from his little black notebook to Molly and Jonathan. "Who has the ring?"

Standing on the far left side of the church platform, Tonya gave a silent sigh, wishing she were the bride instead of a bridesmaid. She fingered her sapphire necklace.

Callie and Melissa stood beside her, and all three faced Molly and Jonathan. The sisters had decided to wear floor-length skirts to practice for their bridesmaid dresses tomorrow. Tonya glanced down at the creamy yellow dress she wore. She loved the way the silky fabric swirled around her legs when she walked. Tomorrow the bridesmaids would wear the fuchsia dresses she and Mom had sewn, with pearl necklaces Molly had given them.

Derek, Ryan, and Murray comprised the groomsmen. Murray stood on the far right and wore the elevator shoes. He was three inches taller than usual, but still, he only came up to Ryan's chin.

Tonya hadn't seen Murray since their "disastrous date" on Tuesday night. That's what she called it, even though the only disastrous part was at the end. When she had poured out her heart to Poe about Murray's law-abiding stubbornness, Poe sympathized and then sided with Murray. In his opinion if she broke the speed limit, she should accept her punishment and pay the fine instead of complaining about it. That was the gist of his thoughts, but he wrote each sentence in a sweet way. Before they parted, Poe softened the entire conversation by saying, "I wish we could talk all night and then watch the sun come over the horizon together."

It was so romantic that she immediately forgave him for siding with Murray.

Tonya dragged her attention back to the rehearsal.

The pastor closed his notebook. "Then I'll say, 'You may kiss the bride.'" He grinned at Jon. "I suppose you could practice that right now."

Jon shyly pecked Molly on the cheek. Callie looked at Tonya and giggled.

"Okay. Now you need to turn toward the audience." The pastor waited while Molly and Jon complied. He raised his voice. "I present to you Mr. and Mrs. Jonathan Hunt."

The opening chords of Mendelssohn's "Wedding March" burst from the organ. Tonya watched Molly and Jonathan leave the platform, followed by Derek and Melissa, and then Callie and Ryan.

Murray smiled as he moved toward her and held out his elbow. Averting her eyes, she crossed to the middle of the platform. He wore a short-sleeve shirt, and she linked her hand through his arm, feeling the strength of his muscle. Together they descended the steps and joined the others. It felt strange to walk beside a taller Murray.

At the back of the auditorium, Jonathan grinned at his bride. "That's a wrap. We went through it twice, so we're finished until tomorrow. Right?"

Adoration lit Molly's eyes as she gazed up at him. "I guess so."

Tonya gave another wistful sigh.

The wedding party, plus parents and extended family, left the church for the rehearsal dinner. At the restaurant, Tonya ended up sitting between Murray and Callie in the crowded room. Derek and Melissa sat across the table from them.

The hum of pleasant conversation surrounded Tonya as she ate her salad. She wished she was sitting next to Poe. Murray made a few comments to her until Derek brought up the recently played Super Bowl. Play by play, he and Murray discussed the entire game. She tuned them out as she conversed with her sisters.

Murray was stuffed. He shouldn't have eaten those last three bites of dessert, although the french silk pie was delicious. If only his partner had been more amiable, but Tonya ignored him during the rehearsal and the dinner.

Still holding a grudge.

Since most of the wedding party and relatives didn't live in Douglas, they formed a carpool to a nearby hotel. Murray entered the hotel lobby behind the Brandt and Hunt families, which comprised at least thirty people. The relatives clumped down the long arm of the first-floor hallway, all rolling their suitcases behind them. Pulling his own suitcase, Murray walked beside Derek, his roommate for the night. Just a few more steps, and he could take off these pinching elevator shoes. He didn't relish the thought of wearing them all day tomorrow.

Following a noisy passel of women, Murray spotted Tonya talking to Melissa. Soon small groups broke off as people found their rooms. Derek stopped at room 127 and slid the card key in the lockbox.

Murray spoke in a low voice. "I'll join you in a few minutes, Brandt. I have to talk to Tonya."

"Sure, Twitch." Derek opened the door and pulled both of their suitcases inside.

Murray walked down the hall as Tonya disappeared into a room with two other women. He strode to the door and knocked.

Opening the door, Tonya looked up at him. "Need something, Murray?"

Only you. "Uh, could I talk to you for a few minutes?"

"Okay." She leaned back in the room to tell her roommates she was leaving, then entered the hallway and closed the door. "What did you want?" She folded her arms.

He glanced down the hallway. Several travelers still looked for their rooms. "We can't talk here, and it's too cold to walk outside."

"Let's go to the breakfast room."

Tonya took off with her long yellow skirt flowing behind her. Murray caught up and strode by her side, ignoring the pain in his feet. They passed the front counter and then the outside doors to the hotel. She entered the breakfast room and led him to a small table in the back. No one else was around.

He took a seat across from her. "This is perfect."

"What do you need to talk about?" She folded her arms on the table. Her entire manner seemed resigned, as if she was at the dentist's office waiting for a root canal.

Murray glanced at the sapphire necklace that resided against the fabric of her dress before he gazed into her beautiful dark eyes. "I just wanted to apologize for the way our date ended on Tuesday night. I realize I was too hard on you."

Surprise swept across her features before she looked down. "I'm the one who should apologize. I talked to. . .a friend. . .about the situation, and he told me to accept the consequences of my speeding ticket instead of complaining about it." She looked into his eyes. "So, I'm sorry."

He tried not to grin, knowing that "friend" was Poe, aka Murray Twichell. "I'll forgive you if you forgive me."

She smiled. "Done. And I really did learn my lesson, Murray. I'm not going to speed down the road anymore."

"I'm glad to hear it." He wouldn't even mention her piano playing. "Can we be friends again?"

"Sure." Instead of getting up, as he thought she'd do, she seemed to relax. "I thought the wedding rehearsal went well, didn't you?"

"Uh, I guess so." Murray shrugged. "Actually, this is the first wedding I've been in, but you're an old pro at weddings."

"Yeah, lucky me. Always the bridesmaid and never the bride."

"You'll have your turn someday." *Maybe I'll be the groom!* That thought startled him. It seemed impossible that they would ever get that far in their relationship.

"Well. . ." She leaned across the table as if sharing a secret. "When I get married, I'm planning to have ten bridesmaids, and I know exactly what they're going to wear. Of course, I must have a June wedding so their dresses will be in the right season." Her voice softened. "I've always wanted to be a June bride."

He grinned, again enjoying this side she seldom revealed. "Maybe next summer, Tonya."

Her eyes widened. "No, *this* summer, Murray. I know June is only four months away, but I'm ready to go. And my dress is going to be beautiful." With a contented sigh, she cradled her chin in her palm. "I designed it myself, and all I have to do is sew it up. Would you believe that Molly is wearing Melissa's bridal gown tomorrow? It's pretty, but I wouldn't want to wear someone else's dress."

"I could finally tell your twin sisters apart tonight." He shook his head. "Never could keep them straight, but tonight I knew who Molly was."

"The one who couldn't keep her eyes off Jonathan Hunt." Tonya stood and pushed her chair under the table. "That's the way it will be with my groom and me—if I find him before June. I might have to get married without him."

Murray laughed as he stood. "I'm afraid he's a fundamental part of the equation, Tonya."

"Yeah, too bad." Her lips curved up as she strolled down the hallway. "The Lord might have to perform a miracle, although I have a guy in mind."

Poe. He ambled by her side, aching feet notwithstanding. What if he ended up marrying Tonya in four short months? Now *that* would be a miracle.

They approached her room, and she stopped to face him. "Tell me, Murray. Do guys care about big, fancy weddings? Wouldn't most men rather elope?"

"Not necessarily." He looked down into her beautiful eyes as she stared up into his. "A wedding is an important occasion since it marks an important beginning—the marriage of two lives into one. Most men want to make it a big day."

"I'm glad to know that." She knocked on the door of her room. "Thanks, Murray. Good night."

He took a step back. "See you tomorrow."

Walking back down the hallway, he heard the door to her room open and close. If only he could reveal himself as Poe. But was Tonya ready to accept him for who he was? What if she rejected him and shut him out of her life?

That scenario scared him. All correspondence would stop. The entire town would discover the identity of her secret admirer—and her dismissal of him. He would be a failure in everyone's eyes.

He paused in front of room 127 as a verse of scripture popped into his mind—something about the Lord holding the king's heart in His hand and turning it whichever way He willed.

God held Tonya's heart. Murray would leave their relationship in the Lord's capable hands. He was thankful he had followed his impulse to apologize. At least he and Tonya were friends once more. For now, that would have to be enough.

ᕤ

Surrounded by other single girls, Tonya lifted her arms, ready to catch Molly's bouquet during the reception the next afternoon.

"Okay, ladies, squish together!" Molly, dressed in Melissa's creamy white bridal gown, turned her back to them and flipped the bouquet over her shoulder.

Watching it spiral toward her, Tonya gave a little basketball-player-like jump and grabbed it. "I got it!" She grinned as the other girls congratulated her. Despite all the weddings she had attended, this was the first time she had caught the bridal bouquet.

Callie ran up and hugged her, their fuchsia dresses

blending together. "Congrats, baby sis! Remember how I caught Melissa's bouquet and ended up getting married the next year?"

"I sure hope that happens to me." Tonya giggled. "But my wedding will take place this June, and my groom will be Poe."

"Maybe." Callie glanced around the reception room and then lowered her voice. "You know, I think Murray likes you. He's certainly been attentive to you today."

Tonya shrugged. "He's making up for the disastrous date we had last Tuesday."

Callie's eyebrows shot up. "You guys are dating?"

"No!" Now Tonya glanced around. Murray stood by the punch bowl talking to Derek. She looked at her sister. "It's a long story, but he apologized last night. We're friends, nothing more."

"I think it's more." Callie leaned closer. "I've seen the way Murray looks at you. He's interested romantically."

Tonya rolled her eyes. "Oh come on. Murray and I never got along, you should know that. We argue all the time." She shook her head. "It would never work. Besides, he's not very handsome. When I get married, I'm going for a hot guy." Tonya's conscience struck her as she thought of her impromptu Bible study Tuesday night. What happened to not looking at the outward appearance? "Well, someone who's pleasant to look at and has a nice personality, too."

"Don't write Murray off, Tonya. He's a good Christian guy. Remember, he wanted to marry me before Lane came along."

Tonya gazed at her sister. "So why didn't you marry Murray?"

"He wasn't the one for me." Callie glanced toward the men. "But he might be the right one for you."

"Thanks a lot." Tonya pursed her lips. Certainly she could do better than Murray Twichell. On the other hand, no one was banging on her door right now, begging to marry her. If she didn't have Poe in her life, she might consider Murray.

Maybe.

sixteen

On Sunday morning, Murray walked into the crowded church auditorium. The service had already started, and he hated being late, although it wasn't his fault. After Sunday school, George Whitmore had buttonholed him, wanting to know the laws concerning domestic violence. His daughter was in a bad marital situation, and Murray had taken fifteen minutes to enlighten the man. Now he needed to get his mind off other people's problems and onto the Lord.

The organ and piano reverberated through the auditorium as Wayne Holland led the singing and the standing congregation belted out the words to "Power in the Blood."

The tempo was much too fast.

Murray wandered down the side aisle, looking for an empty seat. He smiled a greeting to several singing people as he passed the crowded pews. Finally he found an empty spot at the end of the second row just as Wayne seated the congregation.

Murray settled on the pew. Straight ahead he had a perfect view of Tonya Brandt. She sat at the piano, replacing the hymnbook with another music book.

His heart stirred as he gazed at her profile and thought of their instant messaging last night. He had arrived home at five minutes to nine and immediately went to the computer. After all, *Poe* wouldn't have been at a wedding in Douglas all weekend. Sure enough, Tonya's comments showed up at nine o'clock, and they wrote back and forth until midnight.

Pastor Reilly stood behind the pulpit. His shoulders seemed a bit more stooped than usual, but his voice was strong. "Welcome to our church service this morning. We have a lot of announcements, so listen carefully."

Announcements. Murray tuned him out and went back to pleasant thoughts from last night. He kept his eyes on Tonya as he reviewed some of their conversation.

Tonya: *I want to know your identity, Poe.*
Poe: *Sorry.*
Tonya: *Just tell me what you look like.*
Poe: *Picture a fat, bald guy who wears Bermuda shorts.*
Tonya: *Poe! You're not Horace Frankenberg, R U?*
Poe: *Ha! You caught me!*
Tonya: *Tell the truth. R U Horace?*
Poe: *(We had this same conversation over Reed Dickens.)*
    What if I am Horace?
Tonya: *Just say yes or no.*
Poe: *Well, um. . .no.*
Tonya: *Whew! (Big sigh of relief here.) That man is old*
    enough to be my father, plus he has a strange personality—
    unlike you. You're so much fun.
Poe: *We do get along well, don't we?*

Murray had to laugh at that bit of sarcasm.

With the announcements over, the ushers stood in the center aisle, passing the offering plates down each row. Murray pulled two fifty-dollar bills from his wallet, folded them, and threw them into the plate as it went by. Then he centered his attention on Tonya, who played "How Firm a Foundation" for the offertory. Could that arrangement be from the piano book he had given her?

While she played, she kept her eyes glued on the music, and he kept his eyes glued on her. She played flawlessly, weaving around on the piano bench like a cobra to a snake charmer's music.

That girl is so proud. She never moved around like that when she played hymns for the congregation, but as soon as the spotlight was on her, so to speak, she became a drama queen. As the music intensified, so did her hands. She raised them higher and higher, crashing them down perfectly on the right chords every time.

Murray folded his arms. That music must not be as difficult for her as she pretended.

When she finished, the congregation broke out in ardent applause, but Murray didn't clap. Smiling, Tonya glanced around the auditorium. Her eyes stopped at his, and her smile disappeared. Raising her chin a fraction of an inch, she left the piano and walked past him to her seat without so much as a glance his way.

A silent sigh escaped Murray's lips. He picked up his Bible as the pastor approached the pulpit to give the message. *Lord,* he prayed, *I need a word from You today.*

Maybe he should forget Tonya. He loved her on the computer, but in person their relationship was an emotional roller coaster. Of course, it didn't help when he gave her speeding tickets and pointed out her faults.

Pastor Reilly's white hair touched the back of his suit collar as he looked out over the congregation. "Since this is the Sunday after Valentine's Day, we will center our thoughts on love. Our text is taken from 1 John 4:19, 'We love him, because he first loved us.'"

That's your answer. As if the Lord had spoken directly to Murray's heart, he saw the love of Christ to himself—a sinner who didn't deserve God's love. *"While we were yet sinners, Christ died for us."*

And that was the exact love he needed to show Tonya. Love that gives and doesn't expect anything in return. Love that wouldn't be turned off by any angry retort, a cold shoulder, or a proud look. Love that keeps on loving, no matter what.

Murray closed his eyes. *I'll try, Lord.* He would show Tonya the love of Christ, and deep down inside he hoped she responded because now he knew. . .

As crazy as it seemed, he was falling in love with her.

❧

Tonya : *I'm going to a cooking show this Friday in Denver.*

Tonya hit RETURN on her computer and sat back to wait for Poe's reply. It was Monday evening, and even though it was only nine o'clock, she was completely ready to go to bed. She and Poe usually kept IMing until midnight, when she could barely keep her eyes open.

Poe: *What is a cooking show?*
Tonya: *From the brochure—"a two-hour showcase of cooking demonstrations and creative meal ideas, plus handy cooking tips and fresh seasonal recipes." Sounds fun, huh?*
Poe: *Joyous. R U going by yourself?*
Tonya: *Cheyenne Wilkins, Laurie Smullens, and Gretchen Hughes are also going. We're planning to drive down in my car early Friday morning. I'm so excited. Not only will we take home a dozen recipe cards, but everyone will receive a set of measuring cups as a gift.*
Poe: *Woo-hoo! Measuring cups. Every woman's fantasy dream.*

She huffed out a breath. Men!

Tonya: *You could at least be happy for me.*
Poe: *JK—it sounds like your kind of thing, and I hope you have a great time.*
Tonya: *Here's another secret—I'm compiling a cookbook of recipes I created. Since my brother-in-law, Lane Hutchins, is a famous author, I hope he can help me get my cookbook published.*
Poe: *Wow! Sounds great, Tonya. Go for it!*
    A warm feeling filled her. Poe was so encouraging.
Tonya: *At the cooking show they're giving away three prizes— an electric mixer, a new stove, and a trip for two to Hawaii! That grand prize is my fantasy dream.*

Poe: *Don't get your hopes up.*
Tonya: *I know.*

She sighed. It would be amazing if she won anything. On the other hand, it really didn't matter. The cooking show would be exciting enough.

Poe: *What kind of recipes are you putting in your book?*

She shared her ideas with him, dominating cyberspace for half an hour. His comments were few and short.

Tonya: *Am I boring you?*
Poe: *No way. I'm interested in anything that interests you. I want to know all about you.*
Tonya: *Really?*
Poe: *Yes. I have to admit—I'm falling in love with you, Tonya Brandt.*

Drawing in a sharp breath, she sat back. Poe was falling in love with her? But did she love him? She didn't even know who he was!

Tonya: *Are you serious?*
Poe: *I wouldn't tell you I love you unless I was serious. Since we've been IMing, I feel I know your heart—the real Tonya.*
Tears pricked her eyes.
Tonya: *Thank you, Poe. That means a lot to me.*
Poe: *Hey, let's pick out a poem. It will be "our poem."*
Tonya: *My favorite is "How Do I Love Thee?" by Elizabeth Barrett Browning.*
Poe: *Good choice.*
Tonya: *How about a song? Most couples have their very own song.*
Poe: *I'm in favor of "When I Fall in Love, It Will Be Forever."*
Tonya's heart took a leap.

Tonya: *I love that song! But I haven't heard it for years. Do you remember the words?*

Poe: *I'll write out the chorus for you. Hang on, it will take a few minutes.*

Tonya: *OK, I'll wait.*

She couldn't believe this was happening. Poe actually said he loved her! But who was this faceless, nameless guy? Lifting her heart to heaven, she prayed. "Lord, You know who Poe is. Should I tell him I love him?" She rubbed her temples. *I just want to meet him.*

But what if he was "seven shades of ugly"?

Tonya stood and paced to the door. Did it really matter what he looked like? His heart was more important, she could see that now.

"We love him, because he first loved us." The verse from the pastor's Sunday sermon jumped into her mind. The Lord had loved her first, before she loved Him. It was the same with Poe. He became her secret admirer and loved her first, and now she was loving him back.

Poe's reply came on screen, and she leaned forward to read the words of the song, letting the tune run through her mind. With a wistful sigh, she prayed that those words would be true for them—falling in love forever, giving their hearts to each other completely. Yes, that was what she wanted.

Tonya: *That's a great song, Poe, with a message of commitment. But how can we be committed to each other if we never meet? Our relationship can only progress so far on the computer.*

Poe: *I know, but if you met me, you'd be disappointed.*

Tonya: *Disappointed? I'm disappointed you don't want to get together in person.*

Poe: *I'll think about it. So, we have a poem and a song. How about our very own scripture verse? Do you have a suggestion?*

"Man looketh on the outward appearance. . ." Tonya shook her head. That wasn't a good "couples" verse. Besides, she didn't even know what Poe's appearance looked like.

Tonya: *Well, my favorite verse is Proverbs 3:5, "Trust in the Lord with all thine heart; and lean not unto thine own understanding."*

Poe: *OK, and let's add verse six because the Lord needs to direct our paths.*

If only the Lord would direct their paths to each other! But Tonya would have to wait and do what verse five said: Trust in the Lord. Where would she find another man who humbly stayed in the background, wanted to know her heart, and loved the Lord?

Poe was definitely the one for her.

seventeen

On Tuesday morning, Tonya sat at the kitchen table in her favorite blue-flowered pajamas and lilac robe and concentrated her thoughts on a devotional magazine.

It was her only day off this week, but instead of being able to sleep in, Dad had stuck his head in her bedroom at five thirty. "Tonya, get up and make breakfast for Derek and me. We want a hearty breakfast. You know, bacon and eggs—the works."

She did not appreciate her dad waking her, but Mom was in Casper at Grandma's house for a few days, and of course, Dad and Derek could not be satisfied with a simple bowl of cereal.

But now she was awake, thanks to a cup of coffee, and she had everything ready for omelets. She glanced at the counter. Diced onions and green peppers rested on the cutting board along with two tablespoons of cooked bacon bits. Eight large beaten eggs waited in a bowl. Four pieces of bread stood in the toaster, ready for her to push them down. She even had the stove's electric burner on with the skillet sitting nearby.

Now she had to wait for the men, who were out in the barn finishing their chores.

She sipped her coffee as she read the devotion. Today's verse was from Proverbs 31. "Favour is deceitful, and beauty is vain: but a woman that feareth the LORD, she shall be praised."

That was the same verse on the bookmark that her secret pal—Murray—had given her.

The outside door opened, and she heard Dad's voice in the mudroom. Two pairs of boots stomped off snow as the male voices carried on their conversation.

Standing, Tonya walked to the stove. She placed the skillet on the hot burner and whipped up the eggs.

The back door opened. "I'll get that information for you." Dad strode through the kitchen and into the dining room. "Be right back."

Tonya poured the eggs into the pan.

"Good morning, Tonya."

At the baritone voice, she almost dropped the bowl. "Murray?" What was he doing here? She glanced around, and then, realizing she had on no makeup and her hair was a mess, she turned her back on him.

He walked up beside her, and she could feel his eyes on her profile. "Tonya? Are you all right?"

She turned her face away. "Don't look at me! I look awful."

"Awful? Why?"

Tonya tilted the pan. "I don't have any makeup on."

Murray reached out his hand and gently tugged her chin so she had to look at him. He met her eyes—those eyes that were devoid of any mascara or eyeliner. Then his gaze roamed her face a second before he let go. "You don't look awful. Remember when I said you're probably just as beautiful without any makeup?" He grinned. "I was right."

Heat rose in her face, and it wasn't from the stove. "Thanks, Murray." Why did she feel so nervous around him this morning? Callie's words came back to her. *"I've seen the way Murray looks at you. He's interested romantically."*

That couldn't be true, could it?

The back door opened, and Derek entered the kitchen. "Hey, Twitch! Want to eat breakfast with us?"

Tonya held her breath. She'd never survive if she had to sit across the table from Murray with her makeup-less face. *"Beauty is vain."* The Bible verse entered her thoughts and pierced her soul. She bowed her head. *I'm sorry, Lord. Help me not to be vain.*

She turned her head slightly to peek at him. "There's plenty of food here, Murray. You're welcome to stay."

He looked at his watch—the one she had given him at the Valentine's party. "Thanks for the invite, but I have to drive down to Cheyenne this morning."

Dad walked in from the dining room. "Here's that information, Murray." He handed him several sheets of paper. "Let me know what you think."

"I'll do that, Jake." Murray took the papers and moved toward the door. "See you guys later. Bye, Tonya."

"Uh, Twitch." Derek followed Murray into the mudroom. "I'll walk you to your car. I have a question for you."

"Sure."

The men's voices faded as the back door closed. Tonya heaved out a sigh. Why did she care what he thought? Murray—of all people! It shouldn't make one bit of difference. After all, Poe was the one for her.

⁂

Through the snow, Murray clomped beside Derek toward his SUV by the side of the house. Tonya's face stayed in his mind, and what he said was true. She was just as beautiful sans makeup, although he had to admit—with makeup, she was a knockout.

He glanced at Derek. "So what's your question, Brandt?"

"I'm just curious." Derek stuck his hands in his pockets. "Are you interested in Tonya?"

Murray stopped in his tracks. "That's your question?"

"Yeah." Derek grinned as he stopped beside him. "Callie and I were talking the other day, and she thinks you're interested in our little sister romantically. I just wondered if it was true."

Murray looked up at the tall, dark-haired guy. He and Derek had been good friends since childhood, so why not spill his feelings? "Yeah, it's true. But who wouldn't be interested? *Tonya Brandt* is the definition of the word *beautiful*." Murray's breath formed a cloud in the cold air. "But she never pays any attention to me—not romantically. I'm not handsome enough." He grimaced. "She's Beauty, and I'm the Beast."

Derek folded his arms. "Sometimes Tonya's the beast. You should try living in the same house with her."

Murray laughed. "I'd love to, but I doubt if she'd marry me."

"Although, come to think of it. . ." Derek knit his brows together. "She seems to be changing for the better. Writing to that Poe guy has really affected her. Kind of strange, if you ask me."

"That is strange." Murray hid a smile as he turned toward his car. "Well, I guess time will tell, as the old saying goes." He opened the driver's door.

Derek took a step back. "I'll keep this in prayer—about you and Tonya. Wouldn't it be cool if we ended up as brothers-in-law?"

Wow. Murray had forgotten they would be related if he married Derek's sister. "That would be awesome, Brandt."

"We'll pray that way. Tonya could use a steady guy like you." He lifted his hand in a wave before jogging back to the house. "See you later."

Murray got in the car and started the engine. Now both Derek and Callie knew he wanted to marry Tonya. He had always wanted to belong to the Brandt family, but that didn't matter so much anymore. What mattered now was whether Tonya—the woman he loved—would marry him.

At least no one had guessed that he was Poe.

Leaning over, he pushed the buttons on the CD player, hitting the SELECT button until he came to number seventeen. He drove out to the end of the Brandts' driveway before he pushed PLAY. The music of the Hollywood Bowl Orchestra filled the car, and he sang along.

"When I fall in love, it will be forever—or I'll never fall in love. . ."

eighteen

On Thursday evening, Murray left George Whitmore's house on Bighorn Avenue and trudged to his SUV, which was parked on the street. He had spent the past hour talking to George's daughter, Sandra, about domestic violence and the type of things she could legally do to protect herself.

He ran a hand over his face. *Lord, I feel wrung out!*

Gaining the sidewalk, he glanced down the street. The tall, thin spire of his church pointed toward the sky. *That's what I need.*

Leaving his car, he strode toward the white clapboard building. The side door was unlocked, as usual. Pastor Reilly kept it open for the very reason Murray wanted to enter the sanctuary tonight—to have a quiet place to pray.

Walking through the back hallway, he entered the darkened auditorium from the pulpit area and ambled down the middle aisle. He knelt at the last pew on the piano side.

Father, I come before You tonight, lifting up Sandra and her family in prayer.

After he prayed for the Whitmore situation, his prayers turned toward Tonya and himself. Why had he told Tonya he was falling in love with her? That was stupid, even though it was true. But her relationship with "Poe" would never go anywhere. What Murray really wanted with Tonya was a regular man/woman dating relationship. He wanted to marry her.

But would she accept him?

A noise at the front of the auditorium put his senses on alert. Before he could get off his knees, a light came on. Turning, he peeked over the pew in front of him.

Tonya stood at the piano, shuffling some music. The light illuminated her, causing her dark hair to shine as she took a seat on the bench. A few seconds later, the sound of the piano filled the auditorium.

Murray eased onto the pew and let the music flow over him.

When peace, like a river, attendeth my way,
When sorrows like sea billows roll;
Whatever my lot, Thou has taught me to say,
It is well, it is well, with my soul.

Closing his eyes, he felt God's peace fill him. And suddenly he knew God's will—he should pursue Tonya. He should ask her out, let her know he loved her. God was directing his path, just as Proverbs 3:6 stated.

Now if only he could convince Tonya.

Lord, I need some confirmation from her. Even though he had peace about this decision, how did she feel about him?

The hymn ended, and she played another. As Murray watched her, he frowned. Tonya was weaving around on the bench just like she did on Sunday morning. Maybe it wasn't all for show. Maybe it wasn't from pride—unless she was practicing her weaving just as she practiced her playing. He grinned. Yep, that had to be it. Tonya was practicing her pride.

When she finished the song, he stood. It was time to make himself known.

❧

Tonya lifted the damper pedal as the last chord faded away, and someone began clapping at the back of the auditorium. Startled, her hand flew to her throat, and she jumped to her feet. Walking toward her, a man emerged like a phantom from the shadows.

"Who's there?" Her voice sounded squeaky.

"It's just me, Tonya." Murray came into the circle of light.

She breathed out her relief. "Oh Murray, you scared me." She slid back to the bench as a prick of annoyance hit her. "What are you doing here?"

"Do you know how many times you've asked me that

question?" He took a seat on the front row and looked up at her. "Sorry, I didn't mean to frighten you. Actually, I had a heavy burden on my heart, and I came in to pray."

"Oh." With a twinge of conscience, Tonya averted her eyes. Murray had just as much right to be here as she did, but here she was, judging him. Again. *Lord, forgive me.*

Suddenly she didn't want him to leave. "Let me play a song for you." She turned the pages of the hymn arrangement book. "I'm playing through this book you gave me, Murray. I love these arrangements."

"Good." Sitting back, he stretched his arms out on either side of the pew. "Uh, Tonya, I have a question."

She raised her eyebrows at him. "What is it?"

"Just wondering. . .why do you weave around on the bench when you play a piano solo? You never do that when you play for the congregation."

She thought a moment. "Do you remember Janet Oliver, my piano teacher?"

"Sure. She and her husband moved to Kansas a few years ago, didn't they?"

"Nebraska. Mrs. Oliver told me my piano playing should be visual as well as auditory. She was very outgoing, and she *really* moved around when she played the piano." Tonya laughed. "She played according to her personality. So when I play a piano solo, I try to get into my music and be expressive. I don't want to look like a stick with two hands."

He smiled. "You would never look like that, Tonya."

Her face warmed, and she creased the pages of her book. She'd better start playing before he said something romantic, although she was beginning to like his attention. "This hymn is called 'To God Be the Glory.'"

She played the marchlike opening, trying not to think about Murray sitting on the pew. But after a few measures, all she could do was concentrate on the music—the running eighth notes in the bass, the chords an octave higher in the treble, the juxtaposition of soft and loud measures that climaxed in a crashing fortissimo chord.

Keeping her fingers on the keys on that last chord, she let the music die away. She lifted her hands and turned to Murray.

He leaned forward, his arms resting on his knees and his hands clasped. She gazed at his auburn hair and her heart stirred. Murray was really a great guy.

He looked up. "That was beautiful, Tonya. You have a wonderful gift."

"Thank you."

He walked to the piano. "Reminds me of something Edna Beazer told me when I was seventeen years old." His eyes met hers. "I sang a solo one Sunday morning, and afterward everyone said what a great job I did and what a good voice I had." He gave a little laugh. "I believed them. I was so proud— and not in a good way. Then Mrs. Beazer said, 'That's a wonderful talent the Lord has given you.'" He paused, tapping his fingers on the piano case. "That really made me think. God had given me my talent, and He could easily take it away. It was a humbling lesson. Since then I've tried to use my talent for God's glory, as the hymn says."

His eyes held hers for a moment before Tonya looked down. She was often proud of her piano ability—and not in a good way. She was proud of her beauty, too. What if God took those gifts away from her?

Murray glanced at his watch. "Guess I'd better get going. It's eight forty-five already."

"Oh!" Tonya hopped up. Poe would be IMing at nine, and she didn't want to miss him. "I didn't realize it was so late."

Murray grinned. "Is it your bedtime?"

"Well, no." She felt her face flush again. What was wrong with her? "I have something to do at nine." She threw on her coat.

"Let me kill these lights, and I'll walk you out to your car."

She gathered her music together. "You don't have to do that, Murray." He would just slow her down, and she might not get home in time.

"I insist." He followed her out the door.

As it was, Tonya didn't get home until nine fifteen. She immediately ran to the computer and booted it up.

Tonya: *Poe? R U there?*
Poe: *Hi, Tonya! Where've you been?*

With a smile, she settled on her seat.

Tonya: *Sorry. I was practicing the piano at church and lost track of time.*

Pausing, she wondered if she should explain more, then decided against it and hit the RETURN button. She wasn't going to tell Poe about Murray.

⋅❧⋅

Murray settled in front of the computer. Good thing he lived in town and beat Tonya home. He frowned as he read her explanation about being late. She didn't mention anything about seeing Murray Twichell. They had stood at her car for ten minutes talking.

Poe: *So, tomorrow you'll be at the cooking show in Denver.*
Tonya: *Yep. We plan to leave before seven in the morning, go to the show from ten to twelve, then spend the afternoon shopping.*
Poe: *When will you return?*
Tonya: *Don't know. We're shopping at the Park Meadows Mall in southern Denver, so it might take a couple hours to drive back to Fort Lob.*
Poe: *Four hours, at least—an hour just to drive through the big city. BTW, don't rush home to IM with me. I have to work Friday night until eleven.*
Tonya: *OK, but I can't IM on Saturday either. The Single Servings are visiting the Pine River Nursing Home in*

Douglas that evening.

Murray had forgotten. A few weeks ago Derek announced the activity in Sunday school. Later Murray discovered it was Tonya's idea, which surprised him. He didn't realize she liked to visit old people.

Poe: *Hey, I'm off work on Saturday. Maybe I'll come along.*
Tonya: *Yes! Please do! BTW, where do you work?*
Poe: *Ha! Classified info.*
Tonya: *Why won't you tell me who you are?*

With a sigh Murray sat back. Tonya was certainly persistent. He thought back to their conversation tonight at church and knew that Tonya was thawing out toward him. But was she ready to find out that Poe was Murray?

Poe: *You're not ready to meet me.*
Tonya: *Yes I am! If you really loved me, you would do it.*
Poe: *Well. . .I'll think about it.*
Tonya: *You said that before.*
Poe: *I'm still thinking.*

As Murray typed those words, a plan formed in his mind. On Saturday evening, he could sit beside Tonya in the church van on the way to Douglas, stay near her side at the nursing home, and then—as Murray—ask her to attend a play with him at the Cheyenne Playhouse next week.

Their date would be an experiment. He would show her the love of Christ, as well as his own love for her, and gauge her reaction. If they could get through the evening without arguing, and if she seemed romantically inclined toward him, maybe he would reveal himself as Poe.

Maybe.

nineteen

On Friday morning, Tonya picked up Cheyenne, Laurie, and Gretchen in town, and they began their trek to the cooking show in Denver. Although it was only seven o'clock, all four were wide awake and chatting. Not only were they looking forward to the cooking seminar, but they couldn't wait to go shopping.

"I need some new clothes," Gretchen said from the backseat.

"Me, too." Tonya glanced down at her jeans. The blue was fading at the knees.

Cheyenne, on the passenger's seat, glanced back at the other girls. "I only brought a hundred dollars in cash, so I can't buy too much."

"I'm using my debit card, and I just got paid." Laurie laughed. "The sky's the limit for me. I want to buy something special for Corey, too."

Tonya rolled her eyes. "I can't believe you're dating Mr. Hands-on-Me, Laurie."

"Hey, he's been a perfect gentleman. Besides, our names rhyme."

"Corey and Laurie." Cheyenne grinned. "Maybe you two will fall in love."

"I hope so." Laurie giggled.

The conversation swirled around Tonya as she thought back to IMing with Poe last night. Now there was a perfect gentleman, and someone who loved her for herself. As she drove down Highway 270, his words lingered in her mind.

Poe: *Have a great time tomorrow. Win that trip to Hawaii!*
Tonya: *OK, I will!*

133

Poe: *I'm sending my love with you, and you wouldn't believe how much I love you, Tonya. I'll keep you in prayer, too.*

She gave a wistful sigh. She still hadn't told him she loved him, but she knew she did. If only she knew who he was. *Lord, please let me meet this guy!*

But what if he really was Reed Dickens? Poe said he had to work until eleven tonight, and a three-to-eleven shift was common for hospital nurses. Could Poe be Reed? If so, he was certainly different on the computer than he was in person. At church Reed barely acknowledged her, and he wasn't the sensitive, poetic type. No, Poe couldn't be Reed.

At least she hoped not.

But what if she ended up marrying someone else, and Poe just faded from her life? What if she never found out his identity? What would happen to all his talk about love?

Well, she wouldn't give up! She'd keep praying and trusting God to bring them together.

In the distance, Tonya heard a siren. She glanced in the rearview mirror. A Wyoming highway patrol car, lights flashing, rushed up behind them.

"Oh no!" Tonya's shoulders drooped as she pulled over to the side of the road.

The other three girls craned their necks toward the back window.

"Don't worry, girlfriend." Cheyenne touched Tonya's shoulder. "Maybe that cop received a dispatch, and he's going around."

"No such luck," Laurie said. "He's stopping behind us."

Tonya hit the button to roll down her window. "If that's Murray, I'm going to kill him."

Cheyenne laughed. "Murray wouldn't give you a ticket."

"Are you kidding? He's already given me two."

Laurie leaned forward. "Guess what? It *is* Murray."

Tonya tried to quell her irritation, but getting a ticket would take twenty minutes of their time, not to mention another bite out of her paycheck and another spike in her car insurance.

He strode up to her open window and looked inside the car. "Hello, ladies."

"Hi, Murray!" came the reply in three voices.

Tonya didn't greet him. "Murray, I wasn't speeding, was I? I was really trying to stay within the speed limit, and besides that, we're going to a cooking show. We don't have time for this. I don't want to be late."

"Whoa!" He held up his hands. "I'm not giving you a ticket, Tonya."

She looked up into his blue eyes. "You're not?"

He smiled. "You were going four miles over the speed limit, so I stopped you—but just as a warning. The WHP is out in full-force on I-25."

"What's the WHP?" Gretchen asked.

Murray glanced at her. "Wyoming highway patrol." He looked back at Tonya. "They're watching for speeders today on the interstate, so I thought I should warn you. Be careful, and keep your eye on the speedometer." He took a step back and winked at her. "I don't want you to get a ticket."

Her heart fluttered at his wink. "Thanks, Murray."

"Sure. Have a good time, ladies." He strode back to his patrol car.

"That was nice of him." Cheyenne settled back in her seat. "But how did he know you'd be driving on I-25?"

❧

The cooking show was more awesome than Tonya could have imagined. When the girls arrived, they were each given a tote bag full of recipe cards, coupons, and the free measuring cups. The four of them took seats in a large auditorium among several hundred participants, mostly women. A fully functional kitchen was set up on the stage, and one of the cooking masters named Jessie demonstrated a recipe step-by-step. Tonya and the other girls followed along on a recipe card, watching Jessie's hands in a huge mirror hanging above her head and tilted toward the audience. An hour later, they stood in line to fill up on free food samples set on long tables.

With a half hour of the show left, Tonya took her seat in the auditorium. "I guess we won't have to eat lunch."

"I'm stuffed." Cheyenne sat down beside her. "This is so much fun, Tonya. I'm glad we came." She pulled the schedule from her tote bag. "The prize giveaways are the last thing before we leave."

Tonya grinned. "I'm sure we won't win anything, although Poe and I are both hoping for the trip to Hawaii. You know, that would make a great honeymoon package."

Cheyenne raised her eyebrows. "Poe asked you to marry him?"

"No, but I'm trusting the Lord. Someday I'm going to marry that man."

"If I were you, I wouldn't be too quick about that decision. You'd better find out who he is first."

"But he's a Christian, and he's so sweet." Tonya sighed. "Do you know why he's holding off on meeting me?"

"No, why?"

"He says I'll be disappointed. He's 'seven shades of ugly,' or so he says."

"Maybe he's the hunchback of Notre Dame."

Tonya laughed. "I don't think so."

But her smile faded as she thought on Cheyenne's words. Could there be something physically wrong with Poe? Some type of deformity? Maybe that was why he didn't want to meet her.

Tears edged her eyes. Someone as wonderful as Poe should not have to suffer like that. *Lord, no matter what Poe's problem is, I will continue to love him.* She would accept him as he was, deformed or not.

The auditorium began filling up again. Laurie and Gretchen came back and took their seats next to Cheyenne. Tonya stowed her purse and tote bag between her feet, ready to go when they were dismissed. She looked forward to spending the rest of the day shopping at the Park Meadows Mall in southern Denver.

When the audience settled, one of the cooks came to the mic. "Hi, my name is Marcie, and it's time to give away our prizes!"

The audience went wild, clapping and screaming. Tonya screamed with the best of them. She would forget about Poe and enjoy herself.

Marcie waited for the noise to die down. "First, we have a surprise giveaway." She held up a book. "We have twenty cookbooks to award before we choose winners for our three main prizes."

Tonya glanced at Cheyenne. "I'd love to win a cookbook."

Marcie continued, "Open the tote bag you received when you first came in. Everyone has a number posted under the inside flap."

Along with the rest of the attendees, Tonya picked up her bag and looked inside. Sure enough, a small square of paper was wedged under the flap. She pulled it out.

Cheyenne leaned toward her. "My number is 136. What's yours?"

Tonya glanced at the paper. "It's 224."

"My number is 118." Laurie looked at both of them from the other side of Cheyenne. "And Gretchen's is 104."

Tonya smiled. "Let's hope one of us wins something."

On the stage, Marcie turned the handle on a big see-through barrel that was filled with small slips of paper. The other cook, Jessie, joined her as Marcie spoke into the mic. "Jessie is going to pick out twenty numbers for the cookbooks. If I call your number, please come to the front."

The hushed audience waited as Jessie plucked out a paper from the barrel and handed it to Marcie. "Seventy-two."

With a little scream, a woman in the middle jumped up and made her way to the front.

Marcie and Jessie kept the numbers coming, with a steady stream of participants moving forward. Finally Marcie said,

"Here's our last one—number 104."

Gretchen gasped. "That's me!" Her wide eyes glanced at the other three girls.

"Go, Gretchen!" Cheyenne gave her a thumbs-up before Gretchen stood and walked down the aisle. "At least we won something!"

"I'm glad." Tonya grinned. "I wanted to see what kind of recipes they put in their cookbook."

After the participants took their seats, Jessie picked a number for the winner of the electric mixer. Amid the applause, a stout woman claimed the prize. Marcie chatted with her for a few minutes in front of the audience before the lady took her seat.

Marcie looked out over the crowd. "Now Jessie will pick a number for the new stove."

"That would be nice to win," Cheyenne whispered.

But someone else claimed it—a man! Everyone laughed and applauded as he went to the front. Marcie chatted with him for a few moments before he took his seat.

Tonya slipped her number back into her bag. *I knew I wouldn't win anything.*

"Now for our grand prize—a trip for two to Hawaii!" Marcie waited while Jessie picked a number, then she stepped to the microphone. "The winning number is 224."

Tonya's jaw dropped.

Cheyenne grabbed her arm. "Tonya! You won!"

She met Cheyenne's eyes. "I can't believe it!"

Amid thunderous applause, Tonya jumped up and almost ran down the aisle. She couldn't stop smiling. *Poe will be shocked!*

Marcie welcomed her with the microphone.

"Congratulations! What's your name?"

"Tonya Brandt." She took a deep breath and glanced out at the audience. A blur of smiling faces greeted her with more clapping.

Marcie waited a moment for the applause to die down. "So, tell me, Tonya—who do you plan to take with you on this trip to Hawaii?"

Poe was the only person who came to mind. "Well, last night I was IMing with my. . .my boyfriend, and he told me to win the trip to Hawaii, and I told him I would. But I really didn't think it would happen."

Marcie laughed. "So now you can show your boyfriend a wonderful time in paradise."

"Well. . ." She didn't want these people to get the wrong idea. "Maybe this will entice him to propose marriage. After all, a trip to Hawaii would make a great honeymoon package."

"It certainly would!" Marcie turned to the audience. "Give our winner another hand."

Tonya smiled as she walked back to her seat. Imagine winning the grand prize out of hundreds of names! Deep in her heart she knew it wasn't a coincidence. Maybe God was providing the motivation for Poe to reveal himself.

&

At ten o'clock that evening, Tonya passed the WELCOME TO WYOMING sign on I-25. Her passengers were quiet—probably as exhausted as she was. After the cooking show, she had filled out a couple of papers for the Hawaii trip, which was good for an entire year. Then the four of them spent the afternoon shopping. On their way north to Wyoming, they stopped for a late supper at an Olive Garden restaurant.

A half hour later, she exited the interstate at Highway 20. The freeway hadn't had much traffic, but this road looked deserted. After a good twenty miles, she passed the town of Lost Springs, which was more like a building than a town. After all, the sign said it all—LOST SPRINGS, POPULATION: ONE.

She mused on who that one person could be as she drove past a farmhouse off to the left side of the road. A solitary light shone through a window.

Those people are probably getting ready for bed. Tonya wished she could do the same, but from here it might take her another hour to get home. She had to drop off the three girls in town at their respective houses, then drive the seven miles out to the Brandt family ranch.

The orange lights from the dash board illuminated the inside of the car, and soft classical music from the radio accompanied the hum of the engine. With a sigh she rubbed her left eye. That heavy Italian meal made her sleepy.

Suddenly two coyotes dashed across the road in front of her car.

With a gasp Tonya swerved to the left. The car plunged into the roadside ditch. Tonya's left arm smacked against the window, and her face hit the glass.

Then everything went black.

ॐ

Murray received the dispatch at 10:48—twelve minutes before he was scheduled to go off duty. An accident on Highway 20? *Must be a drunk wrapped around a telephone pole.*

Turning on his siren, Murray left the town of Fort Lob and sped down Highway 270. As his speedometer reached eighty miles per hour, he thought about Tonya speeding. She was never far from his thoughts.

He turned west on Highway 20. Glancing in his rearview mirror, he spotted Fort Lob's only ambulance far behind him, the lights flashing. Murray turned right and floored the accelerator for fifteen miles until he neared the Whartons' ranch. Ken Wharton had made the call to 911. As Murray slowed down, he vaguely made out a car in the ditch. Four or five people stood on the road above the vehicle.

Stopping in front of them, he killed the siren and switched on the patrol car's floodlights. His heart almost stopped when he saw Tonya's red Hyundai. It tilted into the ditch, the passenger door open.

Breaking away from the others, Cheyenne ran toward him.

He got out of his car. "What happened?"

"I don't know." Cheyenne looked at him with wide eyes. "I was half-asleep, and then all of a sudden we were in this ditch."

"Is anyone hurt?" Murray surveyed the others as he strode toward them. Ken Wharton, his arms folded, stood beside the car. Gretchen and Laurie stood in the middle of the road together, their arms around each other. Dorothy Wharton, a faded nightgown peeking beneath her coat, stayed beside the girls, her arm around Laurie's shoulders.

Murray's scalp prickled. "Where's Tonya?"

"She's unconscious, Murray. We tried to wake her. . . ." Cheyenne's voice trailed off as she twisted her hands together. "The rest of us are okay."

Tonya. . . . Murray stared at the car. He wanted to run to her side, but his feet wouldn't move.

The wail of the ambulance grew louder, snapping him out of his mental fog. The siren stopped as the vehicle pulled up beside Murray's car. Davin Traxler climbed out of the driver's side. "How can we help?" He walked toward them as Joe Fonsino exited the passenger side of the ambulance.

"We have one unconscious." Murray strode to the car and thrust his head inside the open door. Tonya lay slumped against the driver's door, her seat belt lying useless in her lap. "Tonya? Can you hear me?" He reached across the seat and grabbed her wrist. Feeling a steady pulse, he breathed a sigh of relief as he backed out of the car.

Davin glanced inside. "Looks like her seat belt broke."

Murray looked from Davin to Joe. "Are we going to have to drag her out from the passenger side?"

"Let me look." Joe walked down the ditch and surveyed the car. He tried the driver's door.

"There's no way to get her door open on this side."

"I'll get the gurney." Davin walked backed to the ambulance.

"Please hurry." Murray muttered the words, almost to himself. His heart twisted as he glanced at her still form. What if he lost her?

His determination kicked in. If Tonya lived through this, he was going to tell her he was Poe. He would declare his love for her—whether she accepted him or not. And it didn't matter if the whole town knew.

He would keep pursuing her until she married him.

twenty

On Saturday morning, Tonya opened her eyes to stare up at a white ceiling. She blinked. *Where am I?* A headache pounded in her temples.

A middle-aged woman in a white uniform came into view above her. "Hi, Tonya. My name is Carrie. You were in an accident last night, and now you're at the county hospital in Lusk. You have a concussion, so the doctor wants you to stay here a few days where he can keep an eye on you."

"An accident?" Tonya licked her lips. "What about Cheyenne? And Gretchen and Laurie?"

The nurse smiled. "Your friends are fine. You were the only one who was hurt. Evidently your seat belt broke with the impact, and you hit your head against the window."

"Oh." Tonya suddenly noticed her left arm in a blue sling. "Did I break my arm?"

"You have a hairline fracture just above the wrist. When the swelling subsides, your arm will be put in a cast. It will take at least six weeks to heal."

Six weeks? A numbness filled Tonya as Carrie pushed a button to raise the head of the bed. She helped Tonya reposition herself into a sitting position and get comfortable.

Carrie lifted a plastic cup from the small table beside the bed. "Here, drink some water." She waited as Tonya sipped through the straw. Then she left, promising to send in the doctor.

But that was an hour ago, and no one had come. Tonya had plenty of time to think, especially about the fact that she wouldn't be playing the piano for six weeks. She wouldn't be able to work at The Beauty Spot either. It was a good thing Aggie had hired Connie.

142

The events of last night were hazy. Her mind reached back, trying to remember. Something had cut in the path of her headlights, but what was it? Then—nothing. What happened after that?

The door opened, and her parents walked in.

"Mom! Dad!"

"Oh, Tonya!" Her mom leaned over and hugged her tight. "We were so concerned." She stood back and gazed at Tonya, her eyes bright with tears.

Tonya looked up at them as tears filled her own eyes. "I'm so glad you came."

"Wild horses couldn't keep us away." Dad hugged her, then plopped a little brown teddy bear on her lap. "Here's someone to keep you company."

"Oh, it's cute. Thanks, Dad." Tonya picked it up, admiring the bear holding a red heart with the words GET WELL SOON embroidered on it.

"So tell us, honey. . . ." Mom gazed at her with concerned eyes. "How did your car end up in a ditch by the side of the road?"

Tonya blinked. "Is that what happened?"

"You don't remember?" Dad raised his eyebrows. "The other three girls were asleep, and Murray thought perhaps you had fallen asleep at the wheel also."

Tonya's lips parted. "Murray was there?"

Mom nodded. "Cheyenne said he was very concerned about you. I guess it took a while to get you out of the car."

"Then Davin and Joe took you to the hospital." Dad folded his arms. "Murray called a tow truck, waited for it, then drove the other three girls up to the hospital."

"Dorothy Wharton insisted on it." Mom sat down on the chair beside the bed. "She thought the girls were in shock, but by the time they arrived at the hospital, it was one o'clock in the morning." She shrugged. "They were okay by then."

"So Murray took them home?"

"No." Mom scooted the chair closer. "Murray called us and

the other parents around midnight. We all drove to Lusk as fast as we could. The others left with their daughters, but Dad and I stayed here until three in the morning, hoping you'd wake up."

"I woke up about an hour ago—with a splitting headache."

Dad leaned against the wall. "When we left, Murray was still here. He said he was off duty at eleven last night, and he didn't have to work today, so he didn't mind staying."

Eleven. Tonya frowned. Was there something significant about *eleven*? She lifted her right hand and touched her forehead. *Why is it so hard to think?* "I must look awful."

"The left side of your face is bruised." Mom took a closer look. "It's swollen, too."

"Really?" Tonya wished her head would stop pounding. "Do you have a mirror, Mom?"

Opening her purse, Mom pulled out a compact and handed it to Tonya.

She gasped at her reflection. Her face was puffy, all her makeup had been washed off, and deep purple bruises reposed under both eyes. Her left cheekbone was highlighted with purple, too. She groaned. "I look horrible."

"You're beautiful to us, Tonya." Dad smiled at her. "Things could have been worse."

Mom took back the compact. "Get some rest, honey." She leaned over and kissed her. "We'll be back later."

"Okay." Tonya did feel sleepy.

She closed her eyes, and when she opened them again, her parents were gone.

&

Saturday afternoon Murray exited the hospital elevator on the fourth floor, thankful Tonya was awake now. He had called the hospital on the way over, just to make sure.

Last night he had stayed until five in the morning, but she was still unconscious. He finally left, but only after the nurses promised to sit by her bedside and keep an eye on her every second. Now, after a six-hour sleep and a good hot shower—

and a visit to the florist—he felt rejuvenated.

He glanced down at the miniature rosebush in his hand, knowing Tonya would like the tiny pink roses. A plant would be something she'd have to take home and care for. Hopefully it would grow and thrive.

Like their relationship.

He paused at the nurse's station, surprised to see Reed Dickens sitting behind a computer. "Hey, Reed. Is it okay to visit Tonya?"

He looked up. "Oh hi, Murray. Yeah, go ahead. Tonya's had a flood of church people come by. Seems like the whole congregation." He grinned as he motioned down the hall. "Room 415."

"Thanks." Murray strode down the hall. The door was already open, but he knocked before he walked into the room.

"Come in." Tonya raised her eyebrows when she saw him. "Murray."

"Hi." He gazed at her face as she reclined at a forty-five degree angle on the hospital bed. She looked worse now than she had last night. Her left arm sported a sling. Plenty of flower arrangements filled the small room, and a couple of teddy bears kept vigil over them.

He walked to the bedside. "How are you feeling?"

"A little better. I've had a headache all day, but the doctor has me on all kinds of medicine, so it's not as bad as it was."

"Good." He set the plant on the little table. "I brought you some roses."

"Thank you." She picked up the plant and gazed at the flowers. "They're so tiny."

He nodded, thinking he'd have to start "tiny" with their relationship and keep a lid on his feelings for now. "I was really concerned about you last night."

"I heard." Her eyes looked up into his. "Thanks for all you did for me, and for the girls, too. You really went the second mile."

Because I love you. He shrugged. "When you know the people involved in an accident, it's different than business as usual."

A smile lifted her lips. "I guess so."

"Did the doctor say when they'll release you?"

"I have a concussion, so Doctor Kessler wants me here until Monday." She pointed to a chair against the wall. "Why don't you sit down?"

She wanted him to stay! Hiding a grin, he pulled the chair up to her bedside.

Tonya looked down at her sling. "I also have a broken arm. I won't be playing the piano for six weeks at least."

Murray raised his eyebrows. "That's too bad. I'm glad I was able to hear you play on Thursday night."

"I've been thinking about that. Do you remember our conversation? You said God gave you your voice talent, and He could easily take it away." She sighed. "I guess God is punishing me. He's taken away the two things I care about the most—my piano playing and my looks."

"He's not punishing you, Tonya."

"So many people from church visited me today, and they all saw my ugly swollen face. The doctor won't let me wear any makeup at all until I go home." A tear ran down her cheek.

Murray's heart twisted at her pain, and he grabbed her hand. "Hey, don't cry."

"I can't help it." Pulling her hand away, she covered her face. "I look so horrible." Tears fell between her fingers.

"Tonya. . ." Startled, Murray moved to the edge of the bed and pulled her into his arms.

Grabbing his jacket, she buried her face in his shoulder and sobbed. He tightened his grip, wishing he could hold her forever. He hadn't realized her beauty meant so much to her.

Finally she pulled away with a sniff. "Sorry. I'm so embarrassed."

Reluctantly he let go. "You've just gone through a rough

ordeal. Maybe you've been in shock all day, and you're just starting to realize what's happened."

"Maybe." She pulled a tissue from the box by the bed and wiped her eyes. "But it's so hard to let people see me like this."

"Tonya, it's okay. No one is thinking less of you." Gently he ran his hand down her left cheek. "This isn't permanent. It will heal."

"I know." She sniffed again.

He gazed at her, wishing he could tell her how much he loved her. For the first time in his relationship with Tonya, Murray was jealous of Poe.

He stood. "Guess I'd better move along. The Single Servings are going to the nursing home in Douglas tonight, and I want to go with them."

"Oh, that's right." Tonya looked down. "I was looking forward to that."

"I usually visit my mom twice a week. Why don't you go with me next week?"

She looked up at him. "I'd like that. Thanks, Murray."

His heart stirred as their gazes held. "You know, you're still beautiful, Tonya, even with your face all banged up. The thing about beauty is that it's only skin deep. The real person is inside." He spread out his hands. "Just as the Bible says in First Peter, it's more important for a woman to have a meek and quiet spirit than outward beauty."

She sighed. "I know that on paper, but it's hard to put into practice. I guess I just want to keep up my *image*." She gave a little laugh at her pun.

He grinned, thankful she was in a better mood. "Before I go, may I pray with you?"

Her lips parted, but then she nodded.

Bowing his head, Murray captured her fingers in his. "Father, I lift Tonya up to You. Thank You that she wasn't killed in the accident—it could have been much worse. But now we ask for Your healing. Please heal her physically and emotionally, and thank You that You freely give us all things in Christ because You love us, more than we could ever realize. In Jesus' name, amen." He squeezed her fingers before letting go.

"Thank you, Murray." She wiped away another tear. "And thanks for listening to me blubber."

He backed toward the door. "Remember what I said. The real person is inside, and your inward beauty is shining through." With a little salute, he walked out.

Striding toward the elevator, he heaved a sigh that turned into a prayer.

Lord, I love that girl!

ᕽ

Tonya blew her nose. She couldn't believe she had cried all over Murray's shoulder. But it felt good to cry, and it felt good—unbelievable as it was—to be embraced in his strong arms.

She shook her head. Murray, of all people!

If only he were still here, talking to her. *"I wish we could talk all night and then watch the sun come over the horizon together."* She frowned. Those were Poe's words, not Murray's.

Poe! She hadn't thought of him once today!

Of course, he had not expected to hear from her. Last night Poe worked until eleven, and this evening she had planned to go to the nursing home.

She drew her brows down. *Eleven.* That's what she'd been trying to rack her brain about. Poe had to work until eleven, and when Dad said. . .

What had he said?

With a groan, she lay back on the pillow. *Dear Father, please help me get well so I can think.* Her thoughts wandered back to Murray's prayer, and her heart warmed. Murray really was a great guy, a wonderful man. She closed her eyes. *Wonderful. . . man. . .wonderful. . .*

He stayed in her thoughts as she drifted off to sleep.

ᕽ

Murray booted up his computer at 8:55 on Monday night, then paced the room as he waited. He couldn't sit still, neither could he keep the smile from his face.

Tonya had gone home from the hospital that morning, and he hoped she was planning to IM with Poe tonight. When the computer was ready, he typed his first instant message.

Poe: *Hey, Tonya! I heard about the accident—obviously. My heart just about wrenched out of my chest when I found out, and it made me realize how very much I love you. I've been keeping you in my prayers.*

In a few minutes he was rewarded with her response.

Tonya: *Poe! I could not believe the gifts waiting for me when I got home. Thank you so, so much!*

Murray grinned. He had not only sent her a huge bouquet of flowers, but also a card, a poem, and a sapphire bracelet to match the necklace he had given her.

Poe: *You're welcome. It's a pleasure to buy gifts for you.*

He waited for a few minutes. What was taking Tonya so long? Oh, her broken arm, which he heard was now in a cast. She was probably typing with one hand.

Tonya: *Guess what? I won the trip to Hawaii!*

"Whoa!" Murray stared at the monitor. With all the concern about the accident, not one word had been mentioned about the cooking show in Denver.

Poe: *Are you serious, Tonya?*
Tonya: *Yes!*
Poe: *I can't believe it. Congratulations!*

Tonya: *Thanks.*

Poe: *So, when are you planning to go to Hawaii?*

Tonya: *Not sure, but it's good for a year. It would make a great honeymoon (hint, hint).*

Murray sat back. *Wow!* A honeymoon in Hawaii.

He raised his eyes to the ceiling. "Lord, if this is Tonya's confirmation that I should marry her, You certainly aren't sparing any expenses!" He laughed. "Thank You, Lord!"

twenty-one

Late Saturday afternoon Tonya sat on the passenger seat of Murray's SUV as they made their way to the Pine River Nursing Home. Since Murray wasn't on duty, he wore jeans and a button-down shirt with a blue jacket—the same jacket she had cried on a week ago. She took a deep breath, thankful her bruises were healed and she could wear makeup. Tonya glanced at Murray's profile, admiring the dark beard beneath his skin. Was he getting more handsome?

As he drove, Murray told her about the Single Servings visit to the nursing home the week before.

"Twelve people showed up, including me, and we visited all the residents in their rooms." He glanced at her. "Then one of the nurses asked us to sing, even though our piano player was hospitalized. We gave an impromptu concert in the hallway."

Tonya sighed. "I wish I could have come. What did you sing?"

"Some oldies. 'Red River Valley' and 'Bicycle Built for Two.' Songs like that." He grinned. "Then Corey Henning and I hammed it up with 'Who Threw the Overalls in Mistress Murphy's Chowder?' Corey knew the words better than I did, and he's not even Irish."

"Corey sings?" Tonya couldn't imagine that.

Murray shrugged. "He's pretty good. Wayne should enlist him in the choir."

She didn't reply. Laurie claimed that Corey was a perfect gentleman. Tonya couldn't imagine that either, but maybe she shouldn't be so quick to judge people.

It began snowing as they exited the interstate and entered the town of Douglas. Murray turned the car onto the main street, and they passed a shopping center with a string of stores.

She pointed. "There's the Facial Boutique."

Murray glanced out her window. "What kind of store is that?"

"It's a makeup outlet, and I love that place. I haven't visited it for months."

He slowed the car. "Do you want to stop?"

Tonya hesitated. A week ago she would have insisted they stop. But now thinking about buying new makeup didn't thrill her as it once had. Since the swelling had gone down and her face was back to normal, she was thankful for her looks instead of being proud of them.

Perhaps God let the accident happen for that very reason.

"No, I have enough makeup." She glanced at Murray. "Let's go visit your mom."

He shrugged. "Okay."

With a few turns, they entered the heart of downtown Douglas.

Murray cruised by an empty spot at the edge of the curb between two cars. "Guess I'll park here." He threw his right arm across the back of the seat as he parallel parked. "Hope you don't mind walking a couple blocks. The nursing home has a small parking lot, and I can never find a space. I always park on the street."

"This is fine." She watched several people strolling down the sidewalk. "I guess Douglas has a nightlife."

He chuckled. "Yeah, all the restaurants and bars do a hopping business on Saturday night, even in the winter." He cut the engine. "Let me get your door."

Tonya waited while he circled the car. She thought of the easy camaraderie they shared. She was beginning to like Murray—way more than she should. Wasn't Poe the one for her?

He helped her out, and the cold air smacked Tonya as she exited. She wore her winter coat over her jeans and T-shirt, but she couldn't get her left arm in the sleeve with her cast, so her coat was unbuttoned.

"This sidewalk is icy, so be careful." Murray breathed out white clouds in the frosty air as he spoke.

She smiled. "I'll be fine, Murray. My arm is broken, not my leg."

"I know." He grinned. "I just don't want any more accidents."

As they began walking, Tonya reached to pull her coat closed with her right hand. "It's freezing out here." Thick snowflakes floated down and landed on her hand. If only she'd thought to wear gloves.

Murray stuck his hands in his jacket pockets. "I'm sorry, Tonya. I should have dropped you off at the door. I didn't think about it."

"Neither did I, but that's okay."

On the sidewalk, a tall thin man ambled toward them. His old overcoat was two sizes too big, and Tonya felt sorry for him.

As he approached, he leered at her with bloodshot eyes. "Hey, gorgeous. How 'bout my place?"

She gasped.

Murray's arm encircled her waist. "She's with me, buddy. Move on."

"Oh yeah, shorty?" A string of profanity spewed from the man's mouth, along with the foul smell of liquor.

Tonya quickened her steps, hoping the drunk man didn't follow them.

Murray kept his arm around her waist as he glanced back between them. "Too bad I'm not in uniform. That guy might have thought twice. . ." He pulled her closer. "I'm sorry you had to go through that, Tonya."

"It's all right." She shivered. "I always thought Douglas was a pretty decent town."

"Drunks are everywhere. Sin abounds unfortunately."

They reached the nursing home, and Murray's arm slipped off her waist as he opened the door for her. She felt the loss as they entered the warm building.

A tiled walkway led directly to a receptionist's desk, but on either side were two sitting rooms. The one on the left was decorated as a Victorian parlor, complete with blue-flowered wallpaper and long blue drapes at the windows. A baby grand piano sat in the corner.

Wishing she could play it, Tonya gave a sigh. "That's a beautiful room."

Murray raised his eyebrows. "You've never been here before?"

"No, and my sister works here. I wonder if she's working tonight."

"I'll ask." Murray stopped at the desk and nodded a greeting at the dark-haired receptionist. "Hi, Kate. We're here to see Priscilla Twichell."

"I just talked to your mom an hour ago." The woman smiled as she handed Murray a clipboard. "Please sign in. She'll be glad to see you."

He signed his name, then handed the clipboard to Tonya. She glanced at his neat, blocky printing, reminding her of those speeding tickets. But for some reason she couldn't conjure up one spark of anger. She signed her name below his.

Murray handed back the clipboard. "Is Molly Brandt working tonight?"

Tonya leaned toward him. "Molly Hunt."

"Oh that's right." He grinned at her, and she once again noticed his straight white teeth. He looked back at the receptionist. "This is Molly's sister, Tonya."

Kate adjusted her glasses. "I see the resemblance." She opened a folder and perused the paper inside. "No, Molly left at three o'clock, and she won't be working until Tuesday."

"Thanks, Kate." Murray turned to Tonya. "Ready to visit Mom?"

❧

Tonya hadn't seen Mrs. Twichell for five years, since the woman became a resident at Pine River. Murray's mom had always been short with red hair. Now her hair was snow white, and her tiny frame was as thin as a skeleton. When they entered her small room, she was sitting on a rocking chair near the bed.

"Hi, Mom!" Murray bent over and gave her a kiss on her cheek.

"Murray, I didn't know you were coming over this evening." Mrs. Twichell's head quivered as she spoke.

"Well, here I am." Murray motioned toward Tonya. "I brought a visitor."

Tonya leaned over the older woman and took the fragile hand in her own. "Hi, Mrs. Twichell. Do you remember me?"

"Of course I do, Tonya. Murray told me about the accident. I'm so sorry, dear."

"Thank you." As Tonya gazed at the watery blue eyes, she thought of Aggie saying that Murray was the spitting image of Priscilla, and it was true. Same close-set blue eyes, same large nose. Mrs. Twichell was really rather homely, but Tonya had not remembered that. She just remembered the woman's kindness. Murray's words pierced her thoughts. *"The thing about beauty is that it's only skin deep. The real person is inside."*

Tonya smiled. "I'm so glad Murray brought me to visit you."

"I'll get a couple chairs." He disappeared into the hallway.

Mrs. Twichell kept a grip on Tonya's hand. "Molly keeps me up to date on your family. I was so sorry I couldn't attend her wedding, but she shared her pictures with me. It was a beautiful wedding."

"Yes, it was."

Murray came back with two folding chairs. "Have a seat, Tonya." He set up a chair for her, then sat on the other one.

Mrs. Twichell watched them get settled. "Molly is the best nurse here, in my opinion."

"All the nurses here are good." Murray clasped his hands between his knees. "This is a great nursing home."

"Yes, but I wish the Lord would just take me home to heaven." Mrs. Twichell turned to Tonya. "I'm such a burden to Murray."

"That's not true, Mom." He placed his hand on her shoulder. "Don't talk like that."

Tonya nodded. "I'm sure he's thankful you're still here for him."

"That's right. If it wasn't for you, Mom, I wouldn't have any family at all except for the Hunts. But I don't see them very often."

Tonya thought about Murray living alone in his parents' big drafty house. Poe lived alone, too. She had such a big family; she couldn't even imagine living alone.

An hour passed quickly as they talked about Tonya's family, the church at Fort Lob, and years gone by. Several times Mrs. Twichell's thin knee would begin to shake, slowly at first and then more violently. The first time it happened, Tonya was alarmed. But Murray put a restraining hand on his mother's knee, and the shaking slowed.

Finally Murray glanced at his watch. "We'd better go, Mom. Why don't we pray with you before we leave?"

"Please do." Mrs. Twichell reached out her left hand and grabbed Tonya's good hand. She slipped her other hand in Murray's.

He glanced at Tonya, then looked down at her cast. "Okay. Let's pray."

As Tonya bowed her head, she felt Murray place his arm around her shoulders, pulling her into an intimate circle. Listening to his baritone in her ear gave her a feeling of peace and protection. Tears touched her eyes. Murray was a good son to his mom. A good son and a wonderful man.

&

Murray relaxed as he drove Tonya home. Besides that miserable drunk excuse of a man, this had been a good visit. He hoped Tonya was by his side many times when he visited his mom. Hopefully she'd be by his side the rest of his life.

"I'm surprised you didn't want to stay longer." Tonya smiled at him. "I really enjoyed getting to know your mom again."

"You can come with me anytime, Tonya. I just figured you'd want to get home at nine o'clock so you can instant message."

She frowned. "How did you know about that?"

Oops! Just blew my cover! "Um, don't you IM every evening with your secret admirer?"

"Did Derek tell you that?"

Murray wished he could blame Derek, but he couldn't. "No. . .Poe told me."

Tonya gasped. "Murray! You know who Poe is?"

He shrugged. "Maybe."

Leaning across the seat, she placed her right hand on his arm. "Who is he, Murray? Please tell me."

Murray glanced into her beautiful dark blue eyes. Her face was only inches away, and he wished he weren't driving. If only he could take her into his arms. If only he could tell her who he really was. If only she would respond ecstatically.

With a sigh, he looked back at the road. "Sorry, only Poe can tell you who he is. It wouldn't be fair to him if I told you."

She moved back into her seat, and he felt the loss of her warmth. "Okay then. If you can't tell me who he is, can you tell me what he looks like?"

He glanced at her. "What does that matter?"

"Murray. . ." She leaned toward him again. "Is Poe deformed in some way?"

Deformed? "Not that I know of. Why would you ask?"

"Well, he said. . .oh never mind." She sat back. "He looks normal?"

Murray grinned. "As normal as anyone else I know."

She sat back with a sigh. "That's good. I was willing to accept the hunchback of Notre Dame if necessary, but I'm thankful he's not deformed."

Hmm. . . Must have been that "seven shades of ugly" description. Murray glanced at her. "So you really like this guy?"

She smiled. "Poe and I are of one heart and mind. We love each other."

"You love him?" Murray's head spun. Tonya had never said those words to Poe.

"I think so, but I want to find out who he is before I say anything." She frowned at him. "Please don't tell him."

"I won't, but how can you fall in love with someone just by exchanging e-mail letters over the Internet?"

"It can happen. Like Elizabeth Barrett and Robert Browning." Tonya turned toward him. "You've heard of the Brownings, haven't you?"

"Uh, poets?"

She laughed. "Murray, you're so clueless. Yes, of course they're poets. Poe and I both love poetry and music. We picked out our very own song, and now I'm composing a song for him."

"You are?" Murray raised his eyebrows.

Tonya placed her finger over her lips. "Shhh. Keep it to yourself. I want it to be a surprise."

It won't be now!

She looked down at her cast. "Unfortunately, I won't be able to play it for a few weeks, so I'm taking my time with the composition."

"So what's your 'very own song' that you two picked out together?"

"It's called 'When I Fall in Love, It Will Be Forever.' Have you heard of it?"

"Yeah." Murray motioned toward the radio/CD player. "I have an orchestra version of it on CD."

"You're kidding!" Tonya stared at the radio. "Could you play it for me?"

"Sure." Leaning over, he pushed the SELECTION button to number seventeen. "This is just the music. Want me to sing it for you?"

"Yes please! That would be wonderful." With a smile

Tonya settled back in her seat and closed her eyes. "I haven't heard this song in years."

Good thing I practiced! Murray glanced at her beautiful face as the orchestra played the introduction. If he weren't driving, he could gaze at her during the entire song. But a glance now and then would have to suffice.

He waited for the intro, then began to sing. "When I fall in love, it will be forever. . ."

Tonya gave a happy sigh.

If only that sigh were for him.

twenty-two

Tonya: *I found out that Murray Twichell knows who you are.*

She pushed the RETURN button, wishing she could type with more than one finger.

Poe: *What? That bonehead! Did he give away my
    identity?*
Tonya: *NO, he refused to tell me.*
Poe: *Good. OK, I take back the name-calling. Actually,
    Murray's a good guy.*
Tonya: *I agree. We visited his mom and had a nice time.*

But their visit to the nursing home that evening was beginning to bother her. Not the long drive with Murray, and not the visit with his mom. Even their discussion about Poe didn't bother her. What bothered her were the emotions that pierced her heart when Murray sang.

It would be so easy to fall in love with that man.

Murray had a magnificent voice, but that wasn't the only thing Tonya now loved about him. She loved the way he prayed. She loved his strong hands with the square nails, and she loved the dark beard beneath his skin and his straight white teeth. She even loved his blue eyes.

But what about Poe?

She loved his strength of character, the way he encouraged her, the funny things he said. She loved his Christian principles and humble attitude. And he loved her—the real Tonya. He knew her inmost thoughts and desires, unlike Murray. But how did she know Poe was the one for her when she was developing feelings for someone else?

160

There was only one thing to do—she *must* discover Poe's identity.

ò

Murray reread Tonya's sentences. *Whew!* She hadn't guessed. That was rather amazing, considering all the hints she'd had.

Poising his fingers over the keyboard, he hesitated. Maybe he should take advantage of talking about Murray and find out what she really thought about him.

> Poe: *I'm glad you had a good time with Mrs. Twichell.*
> *I was wondering—do you really, really like Murray? Is there anything about him you don't like?*
> He sat back. This would be enlightening.
> Tonya: *If you're jealous, don't be. He cracks his knuckles.*
> Murray raised his eyebrows.
> Poe: *That bothers you?*
> Tonya: *Yes.*
> Poe: *Why? Cause it makes his knuckles big? (haha)*
> Tonya: *It makes him seem arrogant.*

Murray fell back in his seat. Arrogant? Cracking his knuckles was a sign of self-confidence. At least that's how he always felt. He'd better change the subject before she brought up something he didn't want to hear.

> Poe: *Hmm. . .interesting. Now, tell me your hidden thoughts. What are you contemplating right now?*

Figuring it would take her a few minutes to write back, he entered the kitchen, rummaged around in the fridge, and found a can of cola. He carried it back to the computer and took a swig.

He almost choked when Tonya's IM appeared.

> Tonya: *Poe, you MUST tell me who you are. NOW! I've waited patiently, and patience is not my virtue. WHO ARE YOU?*

"Great," he muttered.

Standing, Murray walked to the window and gazed out at his snowy front yard. The skies were clear and several stars winked at him. "Lord, I love Tonya and want to marry her. I know You gave me peace about our relationship, but I'm still scared."

As strange as it seemed, Poe had become a problem in Murray's developing relationship with Tonya. She wanted Poe, not him. It seemed she had built this fantasy man up to godlike proportions. When she found out he was Murray, she would be disappointed.

He slipped back into his seat at the computer.

Poe: *Give me a couple days to pray about it, OK?*

Just thinking about revealing his identity made Murray's palms sweat.

❧

On Sunday afternoon, Tonya walked down the stairs from her second-floor bedroom. Hopefully she could find some luncheon meat in the refrigerator to make a sandwich before she attended the evening church service. She glanced at her cast. Maybe Mom could help her make the sandwich. It was hard to do anything with one hand.

Murray, dressed in his green patrol uniform, walked through the living room on his way to the front door. "Hi, Tonya."

"Murray, what are you doing—" She stopped. Murray was right—she always asked him that question. "Never mind."

He grinned. "Your dad had a computer problem. Didn't you know I was over here?"

"No." She finished walking down the stairs.

"Uh, Tonya. . ." Taking a couple of steps back, he positioned himself in front of her. "I got a couple tickets to the Cheyenne Playhouse for Tuesday night. Want to go with me?"

A date with Murray Twichell? What about Poe? If she kept spending time with Murray, she might put her heart in grave danger—as far as Poe was concerned. "I don't know, Murray. I'd really like to, but I feel an obligation to Poe. He's my soul mate after all."

"Oh." Murray looked down. "Um, I didn't want to mention this, but Poe gave me the tickets." He met her eyes. "He asked me to take you to this play for him."

"What?" Tonya's ire rose, along with her voice. "Why doesn't he just ask me out himself, for goodness' sake?"

Murray shrugged. "He's a big chicken."

"Aargh!" Her right hand curled into a fist. "What is wrong with that man? I wish he would just tell me who he is."

"Give him time. Now how about that play on Tuesday? It's *Singing in the Rain*."

Tonya's lips parted as her anger dissipated. "Really? That's one of my favorites." She sighed. If Poe wouldn't take her out, it would serve him right if she dated someone else. "Okay, I'll go with you."

"Great!" Murray brought his hands together like he did when he cracked his knuckles, but then his hands dropped to his sides. "I forgot, you don't like me doing that."

She raised her eyebrows. "Poe told you?"

"Uh, yeah. We're good friends, remember?"

Her anger seeped back—against Poe! Why was he telling Murray things that she had told him in confidence?

Murray opened the front door. "I'll pick you up around six thirty Tuesday evening, okay?"

"Sure." She waited for the door to close behind him, then sank down to the second stair. What was the big deal about Poe not revealing himself? And why was he sharing their private correspondence with Murray? Didn't he know Murray liked her romantically? After all, he was asking her on dates, not wearing aftershave because it made her sneeze, not cracking his knuckles because she didn't want him to...

Tonya sighed. Murray was just too nice.

❧

On Monday night, Tonya was completely ready for bed as

she IMed with Poe. She decided to test the truth about the squeaky wheel getting the oil. Every evening she would bug Poe and nag at him, no matter how long it took, until he agreed to reveal his identity.

Tonya: *Still waiting, Poe. When am I going to meet you?*
Poe: *Uh, well, let's see. Tomorrow's out. How about never? Is never good for you?*
Tonya: *NO! I want to meet you ASAP. Who R U?*
Poe: *OK. I once heard a preacher say, "faith takes risks," and I guess it's time for the big reveal. I'll take you up on dinner with your family.*

She almost jumped out of her seat.

Tonya: *Woo-hoo! I can't believe it!*
Poe: *Yeah, well, you might be singing a different tune once you meet me. I hope you're not disappointed.*

They kept IMing, and a decision was reached. Poe had other plans for Tuesday night, and he was working on Wednesday. But Thursday night was free, so he would reveal himself then. Tonya invited him over for dinner with the Brandt family that evening.

Now Tonya wished she didn't have to go out with Murray tomorrow night, but she wasn't about to stand him up. One more date with Murray, and then Poe would be hers forever.

❧

Murray drove his SUV up the Brandts' drive on Tuesday night at the end of their date. It was now after midnight. On the way home, all Tonya could talk about was the play and how great it was. He enjoyed the animated conversation. Now she was quiet, probably tired from the late hour, but he didn't want her to fall asleep.

"Um, Tonya, I heard that Poe plans to reveal himself on Thursday."

She turned a smile on him. "Yep. He's coming over for dinner with the family."

"The entire family?" He could just imagine a huge family reunion with all her sisters and brothers gaping at him. Sweat broke out on his hands as he drove.

"No, just my parents and Derek." She held up her broken arm. "Since I'm not working right now, Mom and I will take all day Thursday to get ready. I'm planning to make my brownies for dessert." She grinned at him. "You know—Tonya's Terrific Brownies?"

"That's great." His hands started sticking to the steering wheel.

"I'm so excited." She gave a little laugh. "Can you imagine? I'll finally discover who's been writing to me all this time."

"Yeah, if he doesn't chicken out."

"He'd better not!" Tonya leaned toward him. "Keep his feet to the fire, okay, Murray?"

Fire. That's what it would feel like. He wiped his left hand on his pants.

Parking the SUV, he glanced at the house. The porch light was on, but besides that the house looked dark. Probably Jake, Yvette, and Derek were all in bed. "I'll get your door, Tonya."

Together they walked up the three steps to the porch. Murray's mind was still on the big unveiling. What if Tonya rejected him?

That would be a true identity crisis!

She opened the front door, then turned to him. "Thanks so much, Murray. I loved that play."

"Yeah, me, too. Thanks for going with me."

"Bye!" Leaning toward him, she brushed a quick kiss along his jawline, then ran into the house.

His eyes widened. "Tonya! Come back here!" If he had known that kiss was coming, he would have grabbed her and kissed her back—on the mouth!

He heard her laugh on the other side of the closed door.

"Tonya!" He wanted to shout her name at the top of his lungs, but he might wake up the rest of the household.

With a sigh, he trudged back to his car. Thursday would come way too soon.

&

Tonya lightly ran up the stairs, then entered her bedroom on tiptoe. What had gotten into her? She had kissed Murray Twichell! But she had to admit that the beard under his skin fascinated her. As the evening wore on, she watched it grow darker. She couldn't resist seeing if his skin was as scratchy under her lips as it looked.

It was.

Murray had seemed rather preoccupied until she kissed him. What had they been talking about before that?

Poe.

Poor Murray. He didn't want her to meet her secret admirer. He must figure that Poe was going to marry her. Maybe Murray and Poe had even discussed it.

She sank down to the bed. Wow! She couldn't wait for Thursday to come.

twenty-three

On Thursday evening, Tonya paced the living room, stopping in front of the big picture window to gaze out at the driveway. Nothing. She took another turn around the room.

"Why don't you sit down, sis?" Derek relaxed in the blue chair.

She stopped in front of him. "I'm too nervous." In fact, she couldn't believe how nervous she was. Her legs were actually shaking.

He stood. "Here, you can sit in this chair. Then you'll have a perfect view of the driveway."

"I can't sit." She held her left elbow with her right hand, supporting the cast. She had dressed up for Poe's big night and was wearing the sapphire necklace and bracelet he had given her. A light blue dress swirled around her knees as she paced, and a navy cardigan completed her outfit. She had actually managed to get her casted arm in the sweater sleeve.

She glanced out the window again. *Where is he?*

Mom walked into the living room. She had also dressed up for the occasion, although a yellow-checked apron covered her green print dress. "Derek, could you come to the kitchen? I need your help."

"Okay." Derek glanced out the window. "Hey, I see a car."

"Really?" Tonya ran to the window and peered out. Her shoulders sagged as she watched Murray's SUV slowly drive closer. "Oh, it's only Murray."

"Ha!" Derek fisted his hand in the air. "I knew Twitch was Poe!"

Tonya faced him. "But he's not. Murray said he knows who Poe is." She bit her lower lip. "I bet Poe chickened out, and Murray came to break the news to me."

"Are you serious?" Derek stared at her. "Murray's been in love with you for weeks. I think he got the idea from Mrs. Yvette Brandt the Matchmaker." He winked at Mom. "Remember the secret pal thing?"

Mom's face tinged pink as she turned around. "I need to check the potatoes."

Tonya placed her right hand on her hip. "Murray is not Poe. I asked him point-blank, and he said Poe had to tell me himself who he was." She cocked an eyebrow at her brother. "It's someone else."

"Tonya," Mom called from the kitchen. "You may as well invite Murray in for supper. And Derek, are you coming? I need your help in here."

"I still think Twitch is Poe," Derek muttered as he left.

Tonya glanced out the window, and a sigh escaped her lips. She wasn't going to find out who Poe was after all. Murray parked his car a few yards back on the driveway, but he didn't get out. She waited. Still he didn't move.

What is keeping him?

She opened the front door and walked outside. As she descended the porch steps, a cool breeze lifted her hair. Fortunately, they were in the middle of a warming trend, and all the snow had melted.

Murray stepped out of his car and slowly closed the door.

She walked down the driveway toward him. *Why is he just standing there?* But as she walked closer, a sense of relief replaced her disappointment.

And it suddenly hit her.

Murray had the exact same qualities she loved about Poe, and Murray was a flesh-and-blood person. The last few weeks ran through her mind. When she had cried, Murray held her in his arms. When threatened by a drunken man, he pulled her close. When he prayed with her, he took her hand in his, squeezing her fingers.

And now she knew. She didn't want to marry Poe, that nameless, faceless guy, that man who said he loved her but was too chicken to come out of hiding.

She had fallen in love with Murray Twichell—of all people!

As she walked closer, gazing at his wonderful, in-person face, she knew she loved him. And deep down in her heart, she knew Murray loved her, too. That must be why he looked so nervous. He didn't want her marrying Poetry Lover Guy. He wanted to marry her himself. And she wanted to marry him.

But how could she tell him?

༄

Murray's heartbeat drummed in his chest as he watched Tonya walk toward him. She was beautiful with her dark hair swirling around her in the nippy air. She had dressed up for Poe, and Murray felt underdressed, even though he wore slacks with a button-down shirt and his blue jacket.

He kept his clammy hand on the door handle, ready to escape as soon as Tonya discovered his identity. She would be disappointed, perhaps even angry, when her bubble burst.

"Murray, it's okay." Tonya put up her right hand like a stop sign as she paused in front of him. "I know Poe chickened out, but it doesn't matter."

He raised his eyebrows. "It doesn't?"

"No, really, it's all right." She took a deep breath. "You see, I've fallen in love with someone else, so Poe is off my short list. Another man has stolen my heart."

His lips parted. She had fallen in love? With someone else? He knew everything going on in her life. Who was this other person?

"Murray. . ." She took a step closer and gazed into his eyes. "These last few weeks have shown me what real love is. It's not just IMing on a computer and sharing secrets; it's everyday living, spending time together, talking face-to-face." Reaching out, she straightened the lapel of his jacket. Her hand lingered there as she continued. "I know we've had our differences, and we've argued. Most of the time it was my fault, and I'm sorry. But Murray, you loved me anyway, even when I had an ugly spirit. You loved me, even when I had an ugly face."

Murray's jaw dropped. "You're talking about me? I'm the guy you've fallen in love with? I'm the guy who stole you from Poe?"

She nodded, and tears glimmered in her dark eyes. "I love you, Murray."

Wow! With a whoop, he threw his arms around her and pulled her close. "I can't believe this, Tonya. I love you, too! I love you—warts and all."

Her eyes widened. "Poe told you about my warts?"

"Haven't you guessed by now, Tonya?" He hesitated. "I am Poe."

"What?"

"Yes. Poetry Lover Guy and Murray Twichell are the same person." He shrugged. "I figured you wouldn't date me, so I became your secret admirer. I wanted to discover the real Tonya Brandt."

❧

Tonya could not shut her mouth. She stared at Murray's close-set eyes and got lost in the blue. Why did she ever think he was homely? "You are Poe? The person I've been writing to all these months?"

"One and the same." He gazed at her. "How do I love thee? Let me count the ways; I wish we could talk all night and watch the sun come over the horizon together." He raised his eyebrows, looking a bit unsure. "I hope you're not disappointed, but it was me all along, Tonya. I can't believe you didn't guess."

"I didn't!" She threw her arms around his neck, resting her cast on his shoulder, and hugged him. "I'm so glad it was you."

"You are?"

She pulled back and looked deep into his eyes. "Yes, I am, Murray. There's so many things I love about you."

His gaze dipped down to her lips. "You wouldn't believe how much I love you."

Tonya had been kissed by a lot of guys, but Murray's kiss was indescribably the best she had ever received. When they parted, they were both a little breathless. For a long moment, they stared into each other's eyes until Murray spoke.

"You will marry me, won't you, Tonya?"

She raised her eyebrows. "You're asking already?"

Murray shrugged. "We've known each other all our lives, and you wanted to get married in June, remember? That's only three short months away. Then there's that honeymoon trip to Hawaii." He shook his head. "I can't believe how the Lord provided that."

"I know!" *Thank You, Lord!* "Guess I'd better get busy with the wedding plans."

"I'll ask you more formally later, with a ring, and it will have to be somewhere romantic. I'm quite the poet, you know." He grinned before glancing toward the house. "But first I'll ask your dad for your hand in marriage. Should I be nervous about that? He might say no."

"Are you kidding? Dad and Mom love you. They'll be so happy."

Murray nodded. "I think you're right. In fact, they're smiling at us right now."

"What?" Tonya whipped around to look at the house. Sure enough, Dad, Mom, and Derek stood at the window. Mom had the phone pressed to her ear.

"Great!" Tonya turned back to Murray. "Mom is on the phone. She's probably inviting everyone to our wedding."

"That's good. We won't have to send out invitations." He grinned. "I've already spent a ton on postage this year."

Tonya laughed and grabbed his hand. "Come on, Poe. I'll introduce you to my family."

As they walked hand in hand to the house, peace filled Tonya. The Lord had given her a great gift, a man who exemplified the beautiful spirit of Christ's love. A man who not only loved her outward appearance, but her heart.

Yes, Murray was the man for her—the man who had taught her the thing about beauty.

Recipe for Tonya's Terrific Brownies

Chocolate Layer:
   6 ounces semisweet baking chocolate
   ½ cup canola oil
   ¾ cup sugar
   1½ teaspoons vanilla
   3 eggs
   ¾ cup flour
   ¼ teaspoon salt
   ¼ cup semisweet chocolate chunks

Cream Cheese Layer:
   8 ounces cream cheese
   ¼ cup sugar
   1 egg

Preheat oven to 325 degrees. Lightly grease an 8-inch square pan; dust with flour.

Melt baking chocolate in a double boiler over boiling water, stirring until melted. Remove from heat and whisk in oil, sugar, and vanilla. Whisk in eggs, one at a time. Stir in flour and salt until just blended. Fold in chocolate chunks.

In another bowl, beat cream cheese with sugar and egg. Spread ⅔ of the chocolate mixture in the baking pan; spoon the cheese mixture over the chocolate layer; spoon the remaining chocolate on top. Drag a knife through to swirl.

Bake for 40 to 45 minutes. Insert a toothpick to test. Let cool in pan for 20 minutes for warm brownies that you can eat with a fork, or cool completely for terrific finger-held brownies. Enjoy!

A Letter To Our Readers

Dear Reader:

In order that we might better contribute to your reading
enjoyment, we would appreciate your taking a few minutes
to respond to the following questions. We welcome your
comments and read each form and letter we receive. When
completed, please return to the following:

Fiction Editor
Heartsong Presents
PO Box 719
Uhrichsville, Ohio 44683

1. Did you enjoy reading *The Thing about Beauty* by Donna
   Reimel Robinson?
   ❏ Very much! I would like to see more books by this author!
   ❏ Moderately. I would have enjoyed it more if

   _____

   _____

   _____

2. Are you a member of **Heartsong Presents**? ❏ Yes ❏ No
   If no, where did you purchase this book? _____

   _____

3. How would you rate, on a scale from 1 (poor) to 5 (superior),
   the cover design? _____

4. On a scale from 1 (poor) to 10 (superior), please rate the
   following elements.

   ____ Heroine   ____ Plot
   ____ Hero   ____ Inspirational theme
   ____ Setting   ____ Secondary characters

5. These characters were special because? _____

_____

_____

6. How has this book inspired your life? _____

_____

_____

7. What settings would you like to see covered in future
   Heartsong Presents books? _____

_____

_____

8. What are some inspirational themes you would like to see
   treated in future books? _____

_____

_____

9. Would you be interested in reading other **Heartsong
   Presents** titles? ❑ Yes ❑ No

10. Please check your age range:
    ❑ Under 18   ❑ 18-24
    ❑ 25-34   ❑ 35-45
    ❑ 46-55   ❑ Over 55

Name _____

Occupation _____

Address _____

City, State, Zip _____

E-mail _____

COWGIRLS DON'T CRY

Journalist Kaleigh McCord is driven by the need to succeed. When the perfect profile story seems to be handed to her with the start of a camp for reading disabled kids on her family's ranch, she jumps into helping—alongside a renowned music artist and a disillusioned pediatrician.

Contemporary, paperback, 320 pages, 5¾₆" x 8"

Please send me ____ copies of *Cowgirls Don't Cry*. I am enclosing $12.99 for each. (Please add $4.00 to cover postage and handling per order. OH add 7% tax. If outside the U.S. please call 740-922-7280 for shipping charges.)

Name _____

Address _____

City, State, Zip _____

To place a credit card order, call 1-740-922-7280.
Send to: Heartsong Presents Readers' Service, PO Box 721, Uhrichsville, OH 44683

HEARTSONG PRESENTS

If you love Christian romance…

$12.⁹⁹

You'll love Heartsong Presents' inspiring and faith-filled romances by today's very best Christian authors. . .Wanda E. Brunstetter, Mary Connealy, Susan Page Davis, Cathy Marie Hake, and Joyce Livingston, to mention a few!

When you join Heartsong Presents, you'll enjoy four brand-new, mass-market, 176-page books—two contemporary and two historical—that will build you up in your faith when you discover God's role in every relationship you read about!

Mass Market 176 Pages

Imagine. . .four new romances every four weeks—with men and women like you who long to meet the one God has chosen as the love of their lives…all for the low price of $12.99 postpaid.

To join, simply visit www.heartsong presents.com or complete the coupon below and mail it to the address provided.